THE ONE

Eden

j. manoa

E

EPIC
Press

Eden
The One: Book #4

Written by J. Manoa

Copyright © 2016 by Abdo Consulting Group, Inc.

Published by EPIC Press™
PO Box 398166
Minneapolis, MN 55439

Printed in the United States of America.

Cover design by Candice Keimig
Images for cover art obtained from iStockPhoto.com
Edited by Ryan Hume

Library of Congress Cataloging-in-Publication Data

Manoa, J.
Eden / J. Manoa.
p. cm. — (The one; #4)
Summary: After Odin learns the truth about the Solar Flare project he becomes
desperate to escape. Odin takes the only action that he believes will allow him to
overcome the hundreds of armed soldiers between him and freedom: he gives control
of his powers to Wendell. With Wendell unleashed, Odin watches helplessly as his
powers are used to carve a horrific path of destruction.
ISBN 978-1-68076-053-8 (hardcover)
1. Imaginary playmates—Fiction. 2. Interpersonal relations—Fiction.
3. Friendship—Fiction. 4. Secrets—Fiction. 5. Psychic ability—Fiction.
6. Young adult fiction. I. Title.
[Fic]—dc23
2015949420

To Daniel Jun Kim, a true hero

1

"Y OU SEEM WORRIED." HER TONE WAS QUIET BUT confident. "Am I distracting you?"

"No," I said, trying to make mine as sure as hers, "not at all."

We sat near the back of the library at one of the four long tables with eight chairs each, set aside for quiet work during study hall periods. I could have sat at one of the individual desks with the raised sides for privacy, hidden between the rows of books, but I didn't like those. They made me feel too shut in, too stuck. I didn't like seeing three big walls keeping me from the rest of the world. It felt too much like being in a box. The tables were always better. They were long enough for entire groups of students to use at once, but the librarians still never let it get too loud. Occasionally students would receive warnings, but after being shut out for the rest of the day after two warnings, most people who valued being in the library learned to be quiet. Those who couldn't be quiet didn't care to be there anyway.

Evelyn and I leaned in from our opposite sides of the table so that no one else could hear. It was like we were sharing a secret. A strand of her hair fell from behind her ear and swept the tabletop.

"Anything wrong?" she asked.

I didn't know what she meant or why she was asking.

"You look . . . uncertain about something."

My Modern American history text was open on the table in front of me. The class was gearing toward an essay exam on the consequences of World War II. Essays required a bit more work than most tests, if only in the physical activity of writing. The text might've been open but in my head I went from World War II to dog fights, to fighter jets, to retracing an old picture book of military aircraft my parents got for me as a kid about a week after the air show we attended at Fort Colton. Between the colorful photos of F15s and F18s leaving vapor trails were various facts: size, speed, engine type, weaponry, dates of production. That book was still on the shelf in my bedroom.

"Actually I'm supposed to be in here practicing," she said, "but instead I came over to bother you."

"It's not a bother."

"Well, maybe you're bothering me then?" she said with a perky grin.

"Hey, I was sitting here first."

"No," she said, "it's fine. I can practice another time." She shook her head, hair flowing freely down like a waterfall in a breeze. Her shaking spread the faint smell of a vaguely flower-scented shampoo.

"Practice?"

"For my audition." She reached quickly into the front pocket of her bag. The smooth line of her collarbone peeked out from the neck of her t-shirt, leading to the one up her neck and then to her ear, small and shell-like with a loop earring in the lobe and a stud at the top. There's a slight redness in the skin under the hair above her ear. A spot of flaky, irritated skin which stood out once I'd become aware of it, like Brent's uneven nostrils. She turned back, a stack of papers in hand. "*Taming of the Shrew.* I'm trying out for Bianca."

She placed the stapled script pages between us. The edges were already frayed and bent from use, the pages creased from folding and curved from rolling. The opening lines of Act I, scene II were highlighted. "She's supposed to hit me here," she said, pointing at the line after the highlights end. "But I don't think that will be included in the audition."

"I dunno. Might help to take one. Show commitment to the part."

"You want her to hit me?" she said, face suddenly that of a puppy left in the rain.

"Kidding."

"Good," she said with a smile, front teeth showing the metal line of the retainer she had to wear that year.

"I hope you get it," I said. "The part, I mean, not the hit."

She chuckled gently. "I know what you mean. And me too. There are like ten other girls trying to be Bianca since this senior Lisa already has Kat, but I should get something. There aren't that many people auditioning overall." Her eyes widened with a sudden thought. "You should try."

I shook my head.

"No, you should," she said with an insistent nod. "It's really fun. You're smart, you have a good imagination. I bet you'd be good at making yourself feel as though something is real. Or real enough to react to it. Besides, maybe if more boys tried out, I'd actually get to play a girl this time." She scowled comically.

I laughed, careful not to be too loud.

The light reflected in her eyes like sunbursts, so bright and close as we leaned toward each other that I could almost feel them burning from her stare. Tiny shadows appear in a triangle of shallow acne scars on the crest of one babyish cheek. I didn't want to look away, but I didn't want her knowing that I was uncomfortable being looked at. I shook my head again, eyes going down to the scratches and stray pen marks on the hard plastic table. "No," I said too feebly, "I couldn't do that. Have a bunch of people watch me like that. I'd feel weird."

She titled her head, expression as welcoming as warm water. "It's not you they're watching. It's the character. That's what's fun about it. You get to be someone totally different. I think that's why every girl actually wants to be Kat. You get to act like a total bitch and everyone loves you for it."

I laughed again. There was something cute about her saying "bitch."

"Really," she said, looking forward in complete confidence, "it's a chance to be someone that you're not. Not really, I mean. It's like, I'll never be Bianca, but I can at least pretend to be her for a few hours." Bianca, the one all the guys want. The part fit, even if she didn't know. "The only bad part is knowing that none of it is real."

"That's bad?" I asked.

"I mean, obviously that's acting, making something that isn't real feel that way, but we never get to experience what it's really like to be that person." Her eyes arced slowly downward. "I know when Bianca is supposed to be scared or angry or when she's supposed to be in love, but she doesn't know any of this." She looked up then, quickly, to my eyes. "She just does it." Then she looked away again. "I know everything that's going to happen to her, but for her, she doesn't know any of it. For me, it's practiced; for her it's real." She looked down at her hand on the table, the silver bracelet on her wrist with the little heart and skull charms. "Sometimes I wish I could actually experience another person's life, what it's like to really be them in that moment when they're scared or happy or sad or whatever, actually feel the way they would feel and not myself imagining it." She looked up again abruptly and inched back, a very slight red in her cheeks. "Sorry."

"For what?"

"I'm not really that weird."

I smiled as reassuringly as I could, unsure if that intention was apparent. "It's not weird. I think we'd all like to know what it's like to be someone else sometimes."

"Yeah," she said. She glanced up and down again. The slight smile, the certainty returning. "I know it's not like real acting, but it would be amazing. Actually being another person without pretending or knowing what's going to happen next. That's what I wish I could do."

"I'm not sure," I said, "I guess it depends what they're doing."

"Hmmm . . . yeah, okay." She nodded. "Maybe it's better if it's not *real*. Like, really real. So we won't have to worry if something bad happens, I mean, to the person we're pretending to be. At least with acting, I get an idea of what it's like being Bianca or, like, Lady Macbeth or whoever, without actually going crazy. It's still just, you know, kinda sad that we'll never get to experience that in the same way they do." She stopped and furrowed her brow. "Does that make sense?"

"It does," I said, trying to show my most understanding look. "No matter how hard we try, we never get to actually be in anyone's head but our own."

She smiled. "I knew you'd understand what I mean."

I nodded again, acting like I believed what I'd said, but knowing it was a lie.

"You seem worried, General." My tone is quiet but confident.

He's forgotten what it's like to panic after so many years in a comfortable command position, having other people do his dirty work for him. After all, he's "commanded 1,723 soldiers to their deaths." General Delgado has forgotten what it's like to be in the crossfire himself.

The eight soldiers behind scramble in disarray. They twitch and bumble, searching for some kind of weapon, something stronger than themselves to use against me. They will find nothing. The only weapon left intact is one they can no longer use.

The table between Delgado and me is new and unmarked. There have never been more than two people here. Delgado twists between looking at me and looking at his soldiers. He's leaned back as far as he can in the chair. I lean back as well. No need to whisper secrets here. The thick walls, with McPherson and Rogers right outside the door, cut us off from the rest of the world.

Delgado's breaths are short and quick, like those of a panting dog. He jumps from the chair. He falls back among the soldiers. His eyes are big and dull, not the narrow points they were before, when he was so tough and claimed that he'd "missed" being face-to-face with "the enemy." Now that he's in the moment, the emotion, the danger, he doesn't know how to act.

He wanted to be alone with us. So he will be.

The eight soldiers fly into the ceiling. Helmeted heads hit hard on the concrete. The motion requires no effort from me. I don't even feel my arms move to lift them. Wendell does everything on his own. I let him.

The soldiers are shoved against the wall and dropped to the floor. They don't move except to breathe. They're as easy to toss around as the old toys in the chest back home. Toy soldiers, all of them.

Delgado spins so quickly he could fall over from dizziness. He practically whimpers as his armed guards collapse behind him. His weapons, his only source of courage, his protection, are useless. Unreliable, as he'd accused me of being.

General.

"General," I hear myself say but I don't feel the muscles in my mouth move. I don't feel the breath push out. "How do you feel about the weapon you have created? Does it satisfy you?"

He doesn't turn. He shakes instead. He keeps one eye over his shoulder. The gun on his belt, still holstered, is the size of a twig. His sidearm is now as much danger as the sticks that Andre and I used to find in the street. We'd hold onto the smaller branch sticking out of the bigger one like a handle and shout "*bang! bang!*" at each other.

You wanted to be . . .

"You wanted to be face-to-face with the enemy." The voice is mine, the words aren't. "Here I am. Face me."

He slowly starts to turn. He stares at the floor until the last moment. I can't hear his breathing anymore. He looks almost peaceful, a death row inmate being strapped into the electric chair, knowing exactly what is coming.

"Well, General, happy about what you have done?"

"Everything I've done has been to protect innocent people from harm." His voice is like a song, a sad one played over movie credits. "To help them stay innocent."

"People like me, General?"

"You were a sacrifice. A necessary one."

"And so are you."

I see my hand out in front of me. The fingers tense to grip the air. Still I feel nothing. The skin around Delgado's neck tightens. An invisible vice compresses his throat in on all sides. His mouth drops open. He chokes out a long, monotone note.

"No," I say, out loud, quietly. "Don't do this."

Him or us, Odin. This is what is needed.

I—we—step around the table and toward

Delgado. He's held upright, but not on his feet, hanging by the invisible force crushing his windpipe.

"He's helpless," I say. Me, not Wendell.

I am doing what you cannot.

Folds appear as the skin of Delgado's neck pulls to the side. His eyes water as he gags, strangled by the very air his lungs ache for.

"I won't—"

This is necessary.

I feel the slightest tingle of sensation in my fingers. There's the pressure and tension, but my fingers don't move. It's as though something, Wendell, is blocking the signals from my brain to the extremities, the places which Wendell said were easiest to control.

"We need him!" I shout, desperate. "The door has a lock on it, we need him to open it."

All we need is his hand.

"Stop!"

I feel the muscles in my hand flexing. Feels like

I'm pushing against a brick wall. I remember the first day with the concrete slabs, slamming the metal balls against them with no result.

This is what needs to be done. You have shown yourself incapable. Thus I am your only way out. I will do what you will not.

Delgado's head slumps to the side.

"There!" I yell. "He's out! No more!"

Very well. We will play by your rules. But when it is them or us, I will do what is necessary.

I feel every muscle in my hand release. Delgado drops lifelessly to the floor. I remain still and look to see his chest rise and fall.

The walls are thick and there are no microphones or cameras in the living quarters. Outside, McPherson and Rogers stand directly in front of the door facing into the waiting area as other soldiers stand guard. McPherson wondered what the general could want, what's happening, wished they were inside so they could see. Rogers only said that it's not their place to ask questions. Delgado is their superior, that's all they need to know. The usual patrols walked through the hallway toward the mess and the holding cells.

"Aren't you curious," asked McPherson.

"No," replied Rogers. That's when I, Wendell, knocked the soldiers against the ceiling and into the wall. They heard none of that.

I am your only chance to survive, Odin. I know more about your powers than you ever will. I can do what is needed.

"No, I can't . . . I just . . . " I search for the words, the logic, to express why we need limits. I try to explain why restraint is still best, even after Delgado tried to kill me yesterday. He would have done so again a moment ago if not for Wendell's intervention. Why wouldn't he try it again and again, until one of us was dead? So why not let Wendell kill him?

Because . . . I can't. That simple. It is not a possibility. Burnett, Choi, Ben, and Aida may have been manipulating me, building me into exactly what they wanted. But they were right about a few things. There is good, objective good, and there is evil. They didn't want someone with my abilities to be evil. That was the purpose behind everything. I am too strong, too powerful, to be evil.

Delgado has a daughter living with her mother, his ex-wife. She's only a couple years older than I am. Goes to Columbia University, studies International Relations. About a month ago he was in DC and she took the train down to see him. They had lunch at the Pentagon dining room. She commented that she'd expected more from the location. It looked like the food court from every mall she'd ever been to, except for the calorie and fat count listed next to just about every dish.

"This is the headquarters of military intelligence," he told her with a warm smile, an actual smile. "We like to know everything." That has to be the difference between him and me. People, whoever they are, are not sacrifices or weapons.

I'm not a killer and I am definitely not a weapon. I'm better than him.

And those who are superior don't waste their time worrying about inferiors. The lion doesn't concern itself with the flies.

"Why should we waste any extra attention on him or the others?" I say, adopting enough of Wendell's logic. "Let's do what we have to and move on. We're wasting time."

There's the jolt of his laughter.

I understand what you are doing. Fine. Try it your way. Just remember what happened the last time I left you alone.

The day I ran from Choi. The day I ended up here. He just has to remind me.

We easily lift the passed-out general off his feet and carry him along in front of us. We drop Delgado to the ground in front of the big door with the handprint identification screen. I look at the closed entrance to my room, the place I've lived in for these last weeks, several weeks maybe.

There's nothing of mine in there. I shouldn't feel any kind of connection to that place. Yet I still do, slightly, a tinge of longing. It was my shelter. The only place where I wasn't watched or guarded. But it's just an empty space in the world, like millions of others, and the rest of the space around it is dedicated to keeping me there, in the way zoo animals are treated to larger cages dressed like home. The rest of this complex is designed to make me grateful for having even the tiny amount of freedom that room afforded me. I hope to never see that room again.

McPherson and Rogers are still right outside. They'll hear the door open, feel it moving, maybe even turn around to see Delgado passed out at my feet. We need to be quick about this.

I lift Delgado's limp hand. I feel the weight in my fingers and arms, but there's a numbness in the fabric of his uniform, like I'd left my hands in cold water for several minutes. I should push Wendell out completely. Force him to become an observer again. Unfortunately, I need him. He knows more than I do. Outside are several dozen more soldiers, armed and armored, trained to kill in a second. I'm not sure I can handle them. Eight soldiers launched simultaneously into the ceiling. I'm sure that he can handle more.

"Not unless absolutely necessary," I whisper. "All right?"

I will only do what is absolutely necessary.

"Once this door opens," I say, more to myself than Wendell, "act normal."

I feel him lingering there in my head, Wendell and I both wielding some unknown percentage of control over this mind we share and the body it commands. The feeling is like that moment when waking up, becoming aware of the real world, but still dwelling on the dream which ended seconds ago, before it slips completely from memory. We place Delgado's palm onto the handprint identification screen.

The door begins to slide open. With two quick

motions we smash the screen to make it inoperable behind us and shove the general's unconscious husk out of sight down the hallway. I hope neither McPherson nor Rogers want to poke their heads inside or speak to him. Better convince them not to.

I step out as soon as there's enough room between the door and the frame. They turn to me at once. I walk a few steps in front before they can look inside.

"The general?" McPherson asks.

"Inspecting the room."

I start my walk toward the elevator.

"He told me to head back to the lab."

"And the rest of his escort?" asks McPherson, falling in step with Rogers and me.

I hear the door beginning to automatically close.

"Inspection. I'm just following what he told me to do," I say, imagining it's just another day of testing. "I'm just following orders."

Their footsteps are slightly louder than those of the other soldiers patrolling the halls. I make no effort to walk but continue to move as if on autopilot.

"I'm just following orders," I repeat.

Rogers nods. McPherson doesn't react but moves along. We pace down the hall and away from the closing door to the room where General Delgado and eight of their brothers-in-arms lie broken and helpless. Alive, but not much more. Neither of my guards look back.

Acting. In the moment, the emotion, the danger, you make it real.

2

I KNOW THEY'RE ALL LOOKING AT ME. THE GUARDS following, those at the corners, at the elevators as we enter and exit, those watching monitors linked to the cameras spaced throughout the complex, they may not want to make it too obvious, but they are all watching me. They have been since the moment I got here. The only change is that the audience has gotten bigger.

I also know that there's nothing for me to do in the testing lab. I haven't been asked to return, not since my protest earlier this morning, but I don't know what else to do. There are only two places I've ever been authorized to be at this time of day;

one of them is presently filled with an unconscious three-star general and his personal cadre of armed troops, and the other is behind this door with the camera above that I glance up at hoping the guards watching me will open it. If they don't, I'm screwed. McPherson and Rogers will know something is up.

My guards take their places on either side of the door that they know should be sliding open by now. I feel the vision on me from every angle, my two escorts from the front, those posted at the elevator from the back, two at the fabrication entrance from the side, and the cameras looking down on us all. Any move I make here will be seen everywhere.

"What's going on?" McPherson asks, turning toward the door. It's never taken this long.

I do nothing.

"Must still be putting together whatever test you're doing today. Should be fun."

"That must be it," I say.

He turns away, which means he focuses on me in his periphery. Rogers does the same. I tilt my head down and close my eyes. I feel my fingers twitch. It's like a nervous twitch but definitely not involuntary. Not out here. Not with these people watching. Not them. The door begins to open. There isn't the same brightness through the frame that there usually is, but it's open. I breathe out in relief and step inside quickly, not even allowing the gap to widen completely before Wendell and I force it to begin closing.

The lights overhead are barely on. The whiteness of the room keeps it from being dark. It's completely empty with not even Winger staring from behind the glass, or Delgado, of course. Never seen it like this before. Imagined it empty, but never actually seen it. The closest was with Burnett only a short while ago. The emptiness makes it feel so much bigger. The gridded black lines over blank space make it seem like the room was meant to be completed later. A place marker, an empty texture, a green screen not intended to exist in this form for very long, as though there was always supposed to be something that came next.

"What now?" I say aloud, looking at the lines in front of me. It's a life-sized piece of graph paper. In which direction does my line move now?

We keep going.

I look across to the other exit near the observation room. The fabrication area, the path down into the depths of the complex where Solar Flare, the engine-turned-weapon, awaits completion. Delgado said it will be finished with or without my involvement. Burnett said we could still stop it.

I close my eyes and try to focus on her. I know her face, her mannerisms, her voice. What I don't have is a rough location. This makes the search a bit more difficult. She could be back in town, at another base, in her old office if she still has access to it, in DC, or anywhere in between. It's an Internet search with just a name and no other keywords. I focus on the last time I saw her, her warning before the guards took her away. I follow her history from there. She spoke with Delgado and Braxton here. Braxton was here, the same white hair and weak chin that I'd seen from Choi's memory the day I was called into Hauser's office. Burnett and Delgado weren't face-to-face then. They were yesterday.

It was Burnett, Delgado, and Braxton in some room on a level I don't recognize. Delgado accused her of betraying the project, compromising its success.

"She's a traitor and deserves to be treated as a traitor," he said.

"She's a civilian and will be treated like a civilian," Braxton replied. He took a moment of consideration before speaking again. "However, we can't risk anyone going to the press about this. Been too damn many leaks already." He met her gaze a second before looking away. "Pending further review, it's probably best to keep her here until she can be safely transferred."

"Here?" she said. "Where? In detention?"

"A fitting place for a traitor. Give you a taste of what your subject went through."

"Clancy," she said, trying to get Braxton to look at her. "At least get me out of here. At least let me go home."

Braxton conspicuously avoided eye contact. "It'll only be for a short time, Doctor." He gestured to Delgado to take her away. That's when the guards seized her.

They gripped her arms tightly as they traveled down the elevator. She could barely see between the mass of guards surrounding her, a mass of gear and guns, the same view I had on my first day. She moved her view around to see, staring as much as possible at the door to my living quarters, then further down the hall. She walked into the cell before they could force her in. She turned around and gave them double middle fingers as the door closed. She then spun on her heel, slid down the door to the ground, and fell into tears. That's where she is now. Cell Six. The one right next to mine.

<hr>

My eyes open.

I should help her. But that would mean going back the entire way I came and either coming up with an excuse to enter the detention area, or fighting my way into it. Then there's the dead end of the cells themselves, with the only entrance being the one I'd have to fight through.

"We have to get her out," I mutter, more as an ideal than a goal.

No. She is not important. Not now.

There would be guards everywhere by then. Guards and guns and orders to shoot on sight, shoot both of us. I don't know if I could handle that. Not all at once.

"Safer in there," I say.

Yes. She does not want to be near us when we do what we must.

"And what's that?"

Escape.

Fort Colton was above us: Thousands of soldiers, tons of ammunition, tanks, jets, and who knows what else that had been hidden, maybe other complexes bigger than this one. And beyond that, the town where I've already become little more than a fading memory and rumor. That freaky kid who brutally beat half a dozen classmates and then disappeared.

We must go.

Mom's in her office at home now. She's setting a date for a dinner fundraiser for breast cancer research. Andre's sitting on the floor of his room playing a game on his phone. Dad's at his job, his real job. He cycles through websites purporting to have the real truth on how to unlock latent psychic abilities by harnessing up to thirty percent of the human brain. He's starting to grow his goatee back. Many more white hairs this time. How long until he finds out what I've done? They haven't told him much and he hasn't asked. Maybe it's best if he doesn't know. They were proud, they really were. Sad that I had to begin my time here in such a brutal way, but happy for what they imagined it would lead to. They too are idealists.

This delay gives them time to prepare.

Evelyn is standing next to Maria near the elevator outside the Panorama Cineplex at the mall. She's wearing a black skirt and short, black boots. Her back arches to rest her elbows on the railing. She sighs as though bored. Her ponytail brings out the roundness of her cheeks. They're in a circle: her, Maria, Brent, Richard, Teddy, and Evan. I guess Brent got them to come along. They're watching the people walking around in the food court. Richard is next to Maria, lightly brushing his arm against hers. She smiles. Evelyn looks over her shoulder at the people riding the escalator to the level beneath them, then those walking between the Foot Locker, Forever 21 and the Starbucks that used to be a Borders back when I was part of that circle next to the elevator waiting for a movie. That was only last summer. The last summer of my previous life.

They are moving into alert positions. We need to go. Now.

Choi told me they would tear the entire town apart. That's how important I am. If they had done that after a couple of afterschool fights, they'll do much worse after I tossed a general and his guards around like paper dolls. It was tranquilizers and black vans then. It'll be M4 carbines and armored vehicles now. There's no home anymore. Nothing for me out there. Nothing for me anywhere.

Let me go.

"What do you want?" I ask the world around me.

For you to move now. Before they come hunting.

"And after that? After we escape?"

Order.

I shake my head.

I want to save them from themselves.

"I don't even know what that means."

So what do you *want, Odin? What is your goal?*

I look at where McPherson and Rogers remain right outside the closed door, to the crisscrossing lines of the empty, unfinished space around me, to the computers and screens of the observation room. I see myself as a vague shape in the glass, a dull orange in the dim light.

Evelyn turns to see the rest of the group circled from her. Maria stares at Richard with one eye cocked and her arms across her chest just enough to push her cleavage out. Richard struggles to keep eye contact while stumbling through whatever statement prompted that look. Teddy points toward the Chinese restaurant in the food court across the mall floor in front of them. Evan points at one of the two pizza places. Teddy mentions that he's eaten at every place here, all eight of them, and Jade Garden is definitely the best. Teddy argues that Antonio's is way better. Brent tilts his head as Evelyn's view turns to him.

"You okay?" he asks.

"Fine," she says. She takes a moment to think. "Maybe I just have resting bored face."

"Sadly, there is no cure for that condition," Brent replies dryly.

"Yeah," Evelyn says, offering a somber look. "But with your donation of only five dollars a month, we can cure resting bored face within our lifetime."

"Only five dollars!" Brent exclaims, shaking his fists in front of him like a child waiting open his first Christmas present. Evelyn smiles. "Where do I sign up?"

Brent motions to Teddy and Evan. He tells them that for the price of one slice from Antonio's, they can cure resting bored face. They look at him like he's crazy. He reaches out to Richard and Maria as though literally pulling them into the conversation.

Evelyn's laugh is high and melodic. Been weeks since I've heard her laugh like that. Feels like much longer. I've missed it. So harmless and free. This all happened a second ago, as the soldiers began to gather outside the testing lab door.

"I just want my friends to be safe," I say.

They are not.

Evelyn brushes her hair back behind her ear as she laughs. Her eyes go small, almost closing.

They never will be safe in this world. Not as it is now.

She covers her mouth, the little silver heart and skull charms jingling from her wrist.

"I know."

Not with Solar Flare.

"I know." The weapon. The weapon that is only possible because of me. The path is right there, right in front of me. "You always said you were here to help."

I am. I am here to guide. To help you make this world safer for everyone.

Evelyn demonstrates resting bored face for the group, none of whom seem to understand why she and Brent find this funny.

"We need to stop them," I say. "Break the machine, destroy the data, whatever we can."

Yes.

"You will help me do this?"

Of course. But you must allow me to do it.

I know the answer before I ask. "How?"

Let me take control. I am our only chance to survive. Let me do what you cannot.

Control. It's what he's wanted the whole time. It's what they've all wanted.

It is our only choice, Odin. You know it. The only way to save yourself—to save them all—is to give me control.

Guards, maybe hundreds of them, would fire countless rounds per second. It was hard enough handling one. If even a single bullet makes it through, that's it. Headshot. Game over. No respawns.

Teddy checks the bulky watch on his wrist and motions that it's time for them to head for the theater. He and Evan lead on. Maria and Richard touch arms as they walk. Evelyn and Brent follow, drifting away from each other as they continue to laugh like little kids, like Andre trying to tell one of his stories. Andre's laugh was like birds chirping, even more harmless.

I never had a choice. "I will," I say, "I will let you destroy the weapon and do whatever is necessary to get us out of here."

There is no other way. There never was any other way.

"So," I say as I approach the rear door, "can we get through this?" It's similar to the one on the opposite wall. "Make it happen."

I will. I promise.

I hear the hum of gears turning and a door opening, behind me. The other door.

I turn as two distinct pops explode into the air. One hits the wall near me. The other is a nail blazing across my leg. I throw both my hands out. I scream. The soldiers slam against the grid behind them. Their bullets fly into the ceiling. I feel the blood trickling out and down my leg. Other soldiers take aim. I crush their weapons with a thought and fling them back toward the others, maybe ten in total. There's a noise outside the door, a flashing light. Sirens.

Give me control.

I check the wound, a rip in my pant leg, a clean cut across my thigh. My fingertips come back bloody. *Ignore it, ignore all of it.* He's stronger than I am. He always has been. I exhale slowly. Shut out the pain in my leg, the blare of the sirens, the groans of the soldiers. *Let everything go.* I shut my eyes quickly and feel myself pull away. My eyes drop open on their own.

"At last," he says. Out loud. In my voice.

My back is to the rear door. Soldiers are strewn

across the other side of the room, some tossed against the wall, others bounced outside. One of them near the door climbs to his feet. Rogers. He checks for his sidearm. His eyes are red above the dark, sagging skin.

"Now we begin."

Rogers aims his pistol. He fires. His bullet curves sharply into the glass of the observation room. I don't feel the flick of the finger that swings him headfirst into the wall. I don't feel the wound anymore. I see it all. Hear it all. But nothing else. I am an observer.

"Such a waste."

The soldiers writhe on the floor. Seconds until they recover. The rear door starts to open.

"Odin!" I hear from behind me. A shout of struggle and stress.

McPherson crouches on one knee, one hand holding him up, the other hand reaching out. Unarmed. The soldiers around him stir, making sliding motions like the slithering of a snake pit.

"Odin," McPherson says again, "don't."

His eyebrows tilt up in the middle with shadows in the bottom of his brow like half raindrops.

"I will," I hear myself say although I don't say it. "I will do anything I want."

McPherson's head twists completely around. The snap rings through the room into my ears and around my head.

No.

Then I turn—Wendell turns—toward flashing lights, testing equipment pushed against the wall, the automatic doors ahead. I barely hear the testing room door close under the sirens.

No, no.

"It was absolutely necessary," my voice says.

No!

Ahead of me, of Wendell, is the long, open passage. The room is clear. Blowtorches and screwdrivers lie on the floor. Large cables hanging from workbenches.

"This is the first step, Odin."

No. No. No. No.

The word echoes in my head like the harsh snap of bone.

"The first step to a better world."

No. Please no.

He continues on and there's nothing I can do to stop it. I've crossed the line. The last line. There is no turning back.

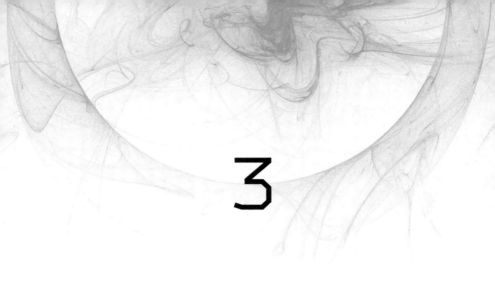

3

CAN YOU HEAR ME?

"Yes," Wendell says. The tone is so familiar it's horrifying.

Why?

"Because you could not." My voice, yet thinner and higher. There isn't the vibration of the sounds in my mouth and throat.

Monster.

"No more than you." This must be how other people hear me.

I would never do that. I would never—

"And that is why it was absolutely necessary," he says. "To show you what has to be done. You were never capable of doing what is required to salvage this world, or the people in it."

It must have been no more than a minute ago that this passageway was abandoned. Maybe that's when the sirens and flashing lights started. Emergency, drop everything. There is a monster on the loose. A frenzy could be happening right outside this room as the mobs rush toward the exits, the ones I've never seen but know are there.

I hear my footsteps—Wendell's footsteps—as a muffled tap on the concrete floor. My view sways with every motion, more than usual, or maybe it just seems that way. What I don't sense is the ground itself, the impact of each footfall, the lift and stretch and step of every motion forward. Feels like one of those first person games Brent and David were always going on about. There's sight, sound, and motion, everything which makes the experience seem real, but nothing solid. No feeling. Not even the burning sensation of the bullet graze on my leg. Not even the leg. Feels like a game where I'm not the player. I've handed control to someone else. All I get to do is watch. And it's terrifying.

"I tried to help you, Odin. I tried to help you understand who these people really are. Their flawed and destructive nature. But you refused to see that."

Here, in this room, as the lights cut in three quick blinks before a sustained flash and the sirens emit a single undulating tone, everything is still. I can tune out the sight and sound if I want now. Literally. I can ignore it, make it seem less real, but that doesn't change anything. I could mentally curl into a ball, try to shut out the rest of the world. The world would go on. Wendell would go on. Ignoring the facts won't make them go away.

"You never had any idea how powerful you were. If only you had let go of your doubts and limits. If you had embraced your power as you should have, perhaps it would not have been necessary for me to step in like this."

Every door along the passage wall is closed. The blinking lights illuminate the emptiness behind the windows looking between this room and the next. Chairs are pushed out from computer terminals. Coats and bags are left on desks. A stack of paper blows away from an oscillating desk fan. Steam drifts from a coffee cup next to a half-eaten sandwich. Not a soul remains.

"That is the true difference between the weak and the strong," he says, coolly, like a teacher to a failing student. "Not abilities. Not money or talent or intelligence. Will, Odin. Doing what no one else can."

Wendell's pace through the fabrication area is almost leisurely. I don't even see his arms swing. I see a long length of bar float from one of the scrap piles near the wall. It comes into orbit around him.

"That is the difference between you and me," he says. "I can."

Murderer.

He laughs. I don't feel it.

"Are you still dwelling on that?"

You made me a murderer.

"Seven billion suffering people on this planet and you choose to focus on one dead prison guard."

Other scraps join in rotation. Drill bits, metal slivers, screws, nails, float through my field of vision. His field of vision. They rotate around him like the debris in the rings of Saturn or old satellites stuck in orbit.

"Do you think your captors would have done anything less to you, Odin? They were under orders to kill at the first sign of defiance. Do you truly believe they would have mourned for you?"

It's no wonder this room had been abandoned instead of defended. Projectiles of all sorts: ball bearings, bits of frayed metal wiring, sawed off tubing, all of them potentially deadly in his control. Better to funnel him forward from of the debris than allow him to tear them apart with a box of bolts knocked on the floor.

"These people, your captors, they have no idea who they were holding. His greatest possible contribution to humankind was as an example."

I could barely hold more than one item in my mind at a time while he has . . . perhaps hundreds, all in constant motion yet a fixed place around him. He moves and speaks so calmly. There's no great strain in holding his growing debris field in place. He just does it.

"Sacrifice is not a crime. The real crime would have been to allow someone so small and meaningless to deprive the world of its best hope for order."

You call this order?

"Yes. The only order there is. The order of power. The order of purpose."

Purpose?

"Think of all the people who spend their lives wondering what to do, what to be, where to go. The majority of human life is wasted on such nebulous pondering. Without an actual purpose, they wander, aimlessly searching for one. They hope to find one. They create belief systems to masquerade as purpose. And they fight each other for centuries over what they think is their one, true purpose."

And you're the one to give this to them?

The one length of rebar stands out among the bits and bolts circling in front of him. A metal tube about an inch thick and three feet long. None of the other scraps are more than maybe four inches in length, and most are small enough that I see only a glint in the flashing lights overhead.

"No one else can. They have tried. Emperors and kings throughout history have tried to unite the world under a common banner. This world and hundreds of others. I have watched them. Thousands of variations. Do you know what happens, Odin? War. Death. Struggle, misery, chaos. That is why they need me.

If you're so fucking mighty you should be able to do better than kill those beneath you.

"A death in this world means nothing, Odin. You of all people should understand that. The captor you mourn for, he still lives. He has more lives than you could ever imagine."

He pauses to look over to the huge door on the

side of the wall, then up to the long window of the security room above us. Every camera and microphone leads to a display there. The all-seeing eyes and ears of the entire complex, however large it may be. They too watch and, at times, hear, but have no control.

There could still be guards inside. They could be reporting our movement to those guards I passed in the halls, or those stationed in the base above us. Traps could be set right through any of the doors ahead. That room is their only advantage, albeit a small one. They can see him. He can't see them.

He chuckles. "Let them watch," he says, before striding on.

"Think of it Odin, an entire world that knows its place in the universe. Billions of people who understand they are living but a small percentage of the life they have. Free from the burdens of worry and doubt. Is it not our responsibility to help these people? To make them understand? Is that not what we all want? Understanding?"

How would you know what anyone wants?

"We all want the same things deep down. Life, safety, purpose. I can grant them all these things. All I wish for in return is that they understand their place in this world."

And what place is that?

"Beneath me. Docile and obedient. Peaceful creatures who live inconsequential lives."

The siren cuts off. The room goes completely black. Lockdown. Happens every day at midnight. I can't tell if Wendell has stopped or not. I can't feel his feet move or his head turn. In here, everything is black.

"The starving man will do anything in order to eat," he says. "He will attempt any crime, any atrocity, any betrayal, until his need is met. Humanity as a whole is like this. It will commit any atrocity needed to preserve itself. Even if that means wiping out the entire planet."

There's a high-pitched hum as the emergency power ticks on. Dim light forms lines above us, making the room look lower, but wider. It's like walking into a manmade cave with reflectors showing the way to the exit.

"Yet, who decides which ideas, people, causes, nations, are worth preserving while others are worth destroying? Who gave these decision makers such power when their positions in life are nothing more than a fluke of probability? What have they done to deserve such reverence?"

They could have kept the power off for as long as they wanted. Forced Wendell to remain or reroute. Even ambushed him in this room after the lights went off. They didn't. They want him to continue. He knows they do. I'm sure of it. He picks up his slow stride toward the transport in the rear, obscured in the dim distance, inching closer with every step.

"In my world there will be no such power structures. People will rise and fall according to their own merit. They will no longer waste their lives or those of others chasing something they can never have. They will know their place in the world. They will be a granted a purpose."

What purpose?

"Whatever purpose I grant to them. The only favor they will ever have to concern themselves with will be mine. The only punishment they will receive will be mine. When they are punished, they will know it is deliberate and just. Yet, they will not resent such a punishment because they will know that somewhere else, in some other world, they exist as they ever have."

That's not freedom. That's slavery.

The path grows darker as we approach the end of the passage. A pair of emergency lights spin on each side of the massive plate covering the transport entrance.

"That is safety. No more chaos. No more fear. Even accidents will be determined according to my will. They will not mourn for their loss, for they know that life continues. They are only a small part of it."

They will fight you.

"I would expect no less. It may even be what finally unites them. But in the end they will see the folly of their actions. They will accept their place once they know the truth. Once they understand that they are powerless."

The rotating debris field seems to sparkle in front of him. He stops before the metal plate covering the transport car. The plate looks impossibly large from down here, almost a quarter of a basketball court stuck to a wall. The soldiers must be gathered around Solar Flare by now. That's where they'll make their stand.

He seems to linger while staring at the dark metal reflecting the thin yellow tint of the lights overhead and the circling emergency signals at the corner. Tiny bumps and flaws cast dot shadows across the surface of the plate.

"Death is always regrettable, Odin. Regrettable but necessary. We must accept this if we are to understand order."

He raises both arms. The transport door rumbles slowly upward. The interior cage lags slightly lower behind the plate.

"Order must be brought to this planet if it is to survive."

Death is the opposite of survival.

"Death of some to save many," he says. Lights mark the upper corners of the transport car. Their glow is lost in the darkness between ends. "Salvation requires sacrifice."

He steps into the transport car. His collection of rotating junk encircles him on all sides in a single plane. Planets around his star. He at the center of everything.

The interior gate and exterior plate slam closed behind us.

"For what it is worth, Odin, I too am sorry. I am confident that with time I could have made you understand why my actions are necessary. But extenuating circumstances have forced me to act before you were ready to."

He pushes his hands forward and one leg back. Open palms face outward as though doing a yoga pose. I don't feel the motion. I hear the friction of the transport forced into movement. There is no grease on the floor or inertia of movement. I'm a ghost. A voice in his head. Nothing more.

"I should thank you as well. Without you in this world I would be ordinary. It is only through our connection, you in the world and me outside of it, that we are able to exert control over reality. If only one of us existed, we would be like everyone else. Instead, we have a direct connection to the energy which creates every possibility."

I'm not the anomaly. We both are. We are each the fork and the outlet.

"Be assured that my promise to you remains. I will destroy the weapon."

Solar Flare. The only thing that may be able to equal him.

"Then, I will set you free."

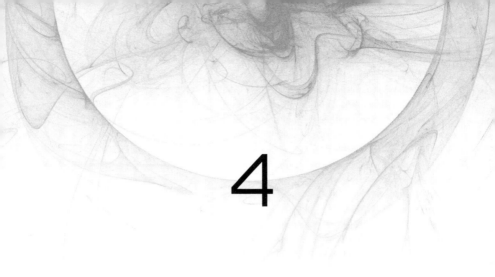

4

THERE'S A LOUD, METALLIC BANG. WENDELL STUMBLES forward a few steps on impact. The screeching of the transport stops. End of the line.

The orbiting debris remains in place as Wendell steadies himself in the stationary transport. I hear him breathe in and out a few times. He closes his eyes and I see nothing but black. He must be searching for someone's memory to access.

It was only a few minutes before the sirens started. Enough time for Delgado and his men to have regained consciousness in the common room and contact others about what happened there. It's weird, I can't see Delgado as clearly as I could before, when I was the one in control. Wendell always could, but for some reason, it doesn't work for me. Still, Delgado must have been the one that signaled for the alarms to sound. There was probably an emergency protocol in place for the evacuation of the complex. That's when the guards, the vast majority of them, would have been positioned to guard Solar Flare. Nothing else is as important as the machine.

Can you see them? How many are there?

"Not enough."

There could be hundreds of soldiers right outside the two gates in front of us. They must have heard the screeching of the transport being force to run and the impact when it stopped. I'm surprised they haven't started firing already, knowing that there is only one person who could have arrived. They'll be far from the door in case it comes flying off at them. Positioned behind something. That's what Brent and David were always going on about during their online matches, idiots not finding cover. Real soldiers would know better. Take cover, aim, wait for the shot. A shot they'd hear and see but never actually feel. The soldiers won't be afraid to use Solar Flare as cover either. There's no chance of accidental explosion. A high likelihood of damage, but a little is better than complete. Wendell has to know what awaits him. Hundreds of soldiers, hundreds of guns, firing hundreds of rounds each. That's why he's remained still the whole time. His plan has to flow perfectly from one thing to the next. There's no time to improvise, not when every second could be his last. His eyes finally open.

You can't possibly stop it all.

I "say" this as though actually speaking.

"Toy soldiers are no threat," he replies, eyes still closed.

The division between us is exactly as he described, I can't see into his head at all. I'm merely along for the ride. Yet, I can't see anything else either, not until he's ready.

Four dim lights in the corner and blackness

in between. Not even the transport's open/close button is lit up. They want to use the dark.

Wendell extends both of his arms out slowly, pushes his palms, plants his feet firmly on the greasy floor, and then yanks back hard. A horrible tearing fills the transport car as the thinner interior gate rips piece-by-piece from the edge of the transport platform. Wendell steps back to give it room as he guides it, the lights on one side placing deep shadows over the horizontal folds which allow the gate to bend as it opens. It's rigid as a board now. He swings it to the wall away from him, covering the forward-most light on that side. All of this while also maintaining the debris field around him.

I have no idea how he's able to do all this. I had enough trouble keeping my little Stonehenge standing. That was many fewer objects and stationary. To actually hold hundreds of tiny bits of metal in constant rotation while maneuvering a huge metal gate. I hate to admit it but he's right.

He's more powerful than I am. Perhaps more than I ever could be.

Wendell steps toward the metal plate hanging over the transport exit. His last protection from what is sure to come. A hail of gunfire. Perhaps even grenades, smoke bombs, rockets, everything they have to stop him. The objects on the very edge of the debris field scrape against the metal plate. I hear the low groan of metal bending. His hands remain out, as though pushing the plate forward. The metal groan grows louder and louder until both sides snap off at once. He holds the plate in front, dragging along the ground, as he cautiously steps from the edge of the transport floor to that of the hangar.

Then come the lights. And the sounds.

The gunshots are loud and constant. One long, sustained static. Bullets hit the metal like thick rain on a tin roof. Banging and rattling. A literal hail of gunfire. One bullet gets through. It flies into the transport behind us. I hear it ricochet. The pops continue. Deafening. Holes open in the plate. Bursts light up in the bullet holes like old flash bulbs. One shot sparks off the debris field.

I'd scream if I could. Just to hear it, to get the blood pumping. Pointless. Observe. Like he did. I would never survive this without him. I had enough trouble turning away Delgado's first bullet, never mind hundreds.

Wendell inches forward. The firing continues. Bullets wearing down the metal. More shots bust through. Wendell pushes one off course. It hits the wall of the transport. The interior gate left there. Sparks pop through the holes in our shield. A handful of screws from the debris field spreads outward. Wendell flicks them through the bullet holes. There are gaps in the gunfire. Silence sneaks in. I hear scattered cries of "Out!" and "Reloading!" Wendell continues to step forward. He holds his hands in front, keeping the wall a few feet away. The gunfire is finally wearing through the metal as more bullets break through. One makes it past the debris field. I can hear the air around it.

Wendell stops moving. He rears back. The metal plate launches into the distance. It slams heavily into whatever they're using for cover. I hear a hollow metallic sound. Several gunshots outline the shapes. Three shipping crates fly across the room.

We are exposed. Shots fly off target. Wendell swings the second gate in front of us. Bullets begin ripping it apart. It bounces off the debris field. I see the shots through the holes. Wendell returns fire with ball bearings and metal shavings. I hear one soldier scream on impact. There are shouts of, "What is that!" "It's still moving!" There is more time between pops. Wendell shifts sideways, away from the transport. He moves into the shadow of the wall. He pulls both arms back and launches the interior gate forward. There is a thin and vibrating crash ahead. Still can't see a damn thing without the light of the gunfire outlining the objects in the room. Better to be dark.

The debris field flattens several feet in front of us. It looks like a metal mesh. Bullets deflect. Soldiers fill in the gaps between the shipping crates. They lean out. Fire. Take cover. Shots bounce off the debris. The impact is like bells striking each other. The debris doesn't move. One shot buzzes passed his ear. Our ear. Wendell draws his hands apart, takes a breath, and claps them together. Two crates screech along the floor. All three slam together. There are screams, crunched bones, and cries of, "Oh my god!" and "Fall back!" He's turned their barricade against them.

All goes quiet. Heavy stomps move away. There is nothing but darkness ahead. Even the debris field is barely more than tiny specks in the dark and one long bar.

There's a scream. One soldier alone fires a string of shots from around the barricade. Most hit the floor. Some fly passed. Wendell launches a nail. The shots stop. I hear the soldier's breath slowly leak out. Wendell throws his arm out as though grabbing for something. The soldier skids across the floor. He stops at our feet, his face unmasked, mouth wide and struggling for air. There's a clean hole through his body armor. Wendell yanks at an apparatus attached to the soldier's helmet, his night vision goggles. The same as those I saw my first day here. The soldier's eyes are big and glassy. His breath whistles. Must have hit a lung. A few shots fire off-line as Wendell secures the goggles into place.

Suddenly the room is a clear field of green and black. The debris of bolts, nails, screws, wires, and sawed off pipe ends is thick and patterned like a fence. Behind it, perhaps a hundred feet away, are the three shipping crates. The center crate is crushed on both sides. Wendell keeps the debris field out front as he sprints forward.

Delgado must not have told these grunts what was coming. Perhaps even he didn't know just how strong Wendell would be. If he did, there would have been many more of them. They would have attempted to blow up the transport before he could leave. They could have collapsed the complex on top of him, on top of us. It's hard to remember that while I'm watching, this is happening to me. This is real. I am in this moment, and there is no way out except to surrender to Wendell's control. He's the only way to survive. I hear boot stomps begin to move around the crates ahead.

The two outer crates fold inward as we approach the center. I hear them clack together once again. He pushes forth. The debris field is intact, a triangle of metal around us.

The crates in front seem to bounce. There is loud scraping and crunching ahead, and crashes of metal on metal—construction materials maybe, or equipment left behind during evacuation. Gunshots echo through the hollow sides. More yelling.

"Flank right!"

"Get behind!"

Not as many shots anymore. Fewer soldiers left.

The ducts stretching from the darkness above come into view. They connect down to the machine. We're getting closer now. What will he do when he reaches the machine in the middle of the room? The soldiers couldn't have had enough time to seal both ends of the tunnel.

There's a crumbling sound and the center crate refuses to move any farther. He closes his eyes for a moment. Planning. Envisioning what he wants to have happen. Eyes open. There is flat green with black shadows ahead, and the ridges of the metal container. The debris field spreads back into orbit. He looks up to see the connecting ducts. We must be at the foot of the machine. We are at the stairs which lead into the heart of the huge metallic tube in the center of the room. It is the size and shape of a submarine. No way they had time to close it. Wendell looks from the ceiling to the floor and back. He launches himself into the air.

"Ugh," he says as he drops onto the staircase

into the machine. Rough landing but on target. He limps forward. Handrails on both sides. A thousand reflections like stars form a circle in front of us. He turns back. There are several holes and a large dent in the crate he vaulted over, and twisted and broken metal cluttered on the floor. I see collected trash, ripped fabric, a hand hanging in the air, a knee bent sideways. Wendell flips both arms up. The shipping crate rolls over the broken parts and slams into the open edge of Solar Flare's entrance.

Then silence. Stillness.

I see myself . . . Wendell . . . in green and black, a thousand times, in the polished surfaces around us. The ridiculously large night vision gear hangs a little too low from the straps around our head. Wendell has to tilt back slightly to see through the headgear properly, like a little kid wearing his father's hat. The debris field is thinner now but it is still there; wires, nails, a screwdriver, the long piece of rebar rotate slowly through my view. Wendell walks on, footsteps echoing lightly on the metal walkway, our reflection rising and falling away in the thousands of angled mirrors lining the interior.

None of this feels real—the green and black night vision, seeing bits of me projected back in every surface on all sides. I don't feel my feet touch the ground or my hand on the railing. This entire event, from the moment Wendell took over to now, feels like a dream. It's like I'm watching an avatar of myself in some unreal world.

Perhaps I'm still in a daze over seeing McPherson's head twist around. That didn't seem real either. Or perhaps it's easier to assume it's not real, that I am watching. Wendell is acting this part as though there were a script prepared and everything that's happening is as it should be. Normal will be restored soon. Whatever normal is.

We progress through four sections of the machine tunnel. Wendell flicks a finger and one screw flies out of orbit. It cuts through several of the reflective metal tiles attached to the machine, making a slight "ting" sound, like flipping a quarter. He makes a bursting motion and more small pieces of debris rattle off into the distance. Still more pop tiny sparks in all directions. Several of the tiles fall onto the pathway, into the nooks of the machine, or hang loosely from the sides.

He stops about halfway down the walkway. The rebar is all that remains of the great ring of clutter that once orbited us. Each section is separated by circular dividers sticking a foot out from the wall all the way around, a little gap in them to allow independent rotation. Far back is the crashed shipping crate blocking the entrance. The soldiers could be trying to cut through it by now. Or they could be praying that whatever it is that just walked through them never comes out again.

"As good a place as any," he says.

For what?

"Brain damage."

He brings both hands up. His palms face in. His fingers spread like a magician preparing to show off his latest trick. There's a series of rapid pops as metal scales pull from their place. They float completely still. A green light bounces off each of them. They almost blend with the rest of the machine. Now the trick begins.

Flashes of light, sparks and tiny explosions, shoot across and through my field of vision. The tiles are whirring blades. They slice through other scales and bore into wires encased in the interior walls. It's all the lights and noise of a Vegas magic show, a dizzying array of blurred motion and fireworks to distract from what's really happening.

Destruction, a near complete tearing of Solar Flare's interior structure.

This machine, made to mimic the electrical process of a human brain, my brain, is being ravaged from the inside. Wendell has marched into my head and dismantled everything about how it works. Nothing remains of what there had been. What had been neat and organized is now jagged and twisted. It's a lobotomy. Wendell has destroyed my mind. And I asked him to do it.

"Happy?" he says, "No more weapon."

I "say" nothing. He has scattered everything I was.

"Now for the second part of our deal."

He walks further into the tunnel. He slowly arches his view around as though he wants me to see the destruction, the stripped bolts connecting outer tiles to the interior walls, the severed wires encased in the beds of the exterior walls, the dented and cracked coverings holding everything else in. Loose parts hang like vines in front of us. He stops between the second- and third-to-last sections of the machine. He waits there. Only the bar remains in lonely stasis, the last of the debris he'd entered the hangar with. It doesn't rotate, it just hovers there at the edge of my vision.

He must be accessing the memory of Burnett leading us—leading me—on a tour through the facility. He wants to see how far back to go for the shortest walk between the machine and the tunnel to Sarsgaard's station. I'm still unsure of Sarsgaard's role, other than famously being an asshole. The external power seemed to be leading into the hangar from somewhere else. I can't be sure without accessing Sarsgaard's memories. I don't know enough of him to picture that, nor do I know the exact location of the power source. Wendell steps toward the division of the two sections.

He digs his fingers into the seam of the thick metal rim running over his head and completely around. He tenses his hands and wrists, veins popping out in his forearms. He's trying to pull the two sections apart, using the space between them to push the metal outward. A low growl rises from the back of his throat. The metal at his fingers begins to stretch, a growing gap of green in the night vision field. There's the crack of circuitry compressing as the casing moves. Wendell pants as he steps back. The two metal rims dividing the sections bend inward. They look like prison bars from old movies where the super strong criminal pulls the bars apart to break out.

The metal rebar clanks loudly against the exposed casing around the machine. In normal light, the outer shell would be the dark green of a sewer pipe. In night vision, it's just black with a few uneven spots of lighter black. Wendell slams the end of the bar over and over until the edge begins to blunt and crack.

"Focus," he mutters. "Focus."

The bar slams into the wall again. The collision echoes through the tunnel around us. It must be loud enough that even the soldiers outside know what's happening. "Come on," he grunts. Another loud clank as the pipe uselessly bashes against the much thicker shell. He stands perpendicular to the wall. He swings his arms as though bailing water from a sinking ship. "The result," he says between breaths, "not the method." There's a loud bang as a small crack appears in the casing. "Yes!" he says loudly, casting the bar away. It's the closest I've ever heard him to be being excited.

He doesn't touch the wall this time. Instead he uses his hands as a reference, like crosshairs or iron sights. The crack in the wall begins to grow. The space between the two sides expands. I can hear the metal ripping on both ends.

I'd never be able to do this. I didn't even know it was possible. This is the way he could have broken me out of the living quarters I'd been trapped in. Maybe even gotten through the vents in the ceiling of the detention cell. Instead I had to remain in those places. A prisoner, when I could have been free anytime. No. This is how he wanted to escape. He wanted to go through the hangar, the machine inside. He must have known the whole time.

The crack in the wall pulls apart like the seam before it. I hear the soldiers taking position right outside the lengthening crack. The same rattle of guns lifting as I'd heard from Rogers and McPherson as I exited the testing room every day.

"Steady," I hear whispered from the sliver opened in the wall. Wendell breathes out slowly. I see his hands pull back in front of him as though preparing for a final push.

With one shove the exterior wall splits open wide enough to walk through. The soldiers fly backward, hit by the same force which cracked the machine. He steps out to the familiar crunch of weapons. The soldiers stare helplessly. Their head gear hangs ridiculously over their eyes. They pull the triggers of useless guns, as dangerous as toy rifles. He tosses all of them away. Other troops run from around the other side of the machine.

There's the door to Sarsgaard's station. Wendell yanks it from the wall. He flings it to the side. Gunshots surround him. He doesn't care. He walks directly into the hallway toward Sarsgaard's room.

Angry voices bounce off the narrow walls in front of us. Hushed voices come from the back.

I hear a metallic object hit the floor several paces behind, and the hiss of gas leaking in the hall. Wendell pulls off the goggles as the station nears. "Hear that?" someone says from inside the room in front of us. There's an electric hum and a glow of yellow light coming from the station.

The equipment inside is running. Computers, monitors, and overhead lights, are all turned on. Sarsgaard and two others freeze and stare at Wendell. Wendell stares back. A female technician staggers away from her computer terminal. A male technician sinks in his chair. Sarsgaard remains standing, shaking, eyes as big as bottle caps but half as solid.

"I . . . I," Sarsgaard stammers. He steps back and almost trips over an office chair. "I . . . "

"Apologies, Doctor," says Wendell. "This is not about you."

With one swing Wendell launches a computer monitor. Glass shatters into Sarsgaard's face. The force carries him into a desk against the wall. One of the technicians screams. Sarsgaard drops to the floor.

Wendell scoffs. "Headshot."

The male technician shakes so violently that a loose screw squeaks under him. The female tech near the back crouches behind the computer bank. Wendell approaches the man in the chair slowly. The man puts his forearms up, covering is face. Wendell leans toward him. "Run," he says, before backing away.

The tech's eyes dart back and forth. The other knocks a stack of papers off a desk as she bolts for a rear door.

"Go," Wendell says. He points at the tech's computer. "I need to use that." The tech stands as though trying to walk through an earthquake, turns, and sprints toward the door. Wendell sits in the chair, the loose screw squeaking again.

Why let them go? I "speak" at last, feeling safe enough here to pull some level of attention away. The soldiers aren't charging in. They must expect us to come back out. The gas never reached the room, as though something were holding it in place.

"You would prefer I killed them?"

Wendell clicks around on the computer screen faster than I can read the options, using someone else's memories to see the positions of the icons.

Of course not, but, why not *them?*

"They were no threat. They had nothing I could not otherwise have."

Sarsgaard was no threat.

"True. But he was a jerk."

The folders on the screen stretch into long branches of technical mumbo jumbo as he scrolls down the screen until he reaches one: Emergency Protocols. The files in the folder are marked with the Greek characters alpha, beta, and omega. He clicks omega. A black and green DOS window appears with *C:\> prompt.*

What are you doing?

"Fulfilling our agreement," he says.

The key strokes are thin machine-gun fire: *248-X76-5640ac2-DRDI142-Ω-exe. Enter.*

Override fail safe C:\>. Wendell waits a moment to find the information. Probably from Sarsgaard. *c23-XX1-67r-ovr:sar.*

Lights flash. A siren wails. A loud rumble shakes the glass broken around Sarsgaard's body.

What the hell did you do?

Wendell says nothing. He stands up from the computer. He looks down at Sarsgaard long enough to see the shattered eye socket, the glass embedded in the forehead, nose, and cheeks, and the blood pooling around pieces of broken glass and plastic. Is that what Kevin looked like under my bag? Face caved inward? Did Wendell want me to see that? Or did he want to see it for himself? The light off the glass trembles. The rumbling grows louder.

Wendell stops at the entrance to the walkway between the station and the hangar. He places his hands out as though preparing to catch something.

The gas remains in a concentrated cloud. The three quick blinks of light continue. The rumbling, hissing, crashing noises from outside cover the undulating siren. Water slides onto the floor of the tunnel ahead. It stops at the door, inches from Wendell's feet. The water grows. One foot high. Two feet high. Three feet high. Rising to the ceiling. Through the hall I see Solar Flare crack. The deluge tosses the machine aside. Wendell waits for the walkway to fill before stepping out.

The water retreats. The ground, walls, and ceiling are completely dry as he strides forward. No flashing lights. No sirens. No rumble, hiss, or crash. Not even a bubble. All is still.

A pocket extends out as Wendell steps into the hangar. A dome forms over us. Shadows drift through the murky water. Solar Flare bends up toward the ceiling. He turns toward the back of the hangar. A shallow light shines through the opened flood doors in the rear wall. Emergency protocol. Destroy everything.

Chunks of broken metal drift by. Bodies brush the edge of the dome. In the distance are the solid, angular shapes of shipping containers, forklifts, a truck, a crane, and other mechanical things. Among them are the rounder shapes of bodies, suspended in the space above and around me. Dead drifting. They look almost peaceful.

Wendell approaches the rear hangar wall, the opening that let the lake in. Tons of debris float by, a whole new collection of scrap with us in the center. Wendell pauses at the end of the hangar floor, just before the sudden drop onto the tracks of the ten-foot-thick walls that held the water back and a gentle incline leading to the river. Light breaks through the river in patches and beams. The gentle white of the sun bounces around the dark water, not the thick glow of artificial lights.

Wendell steps to the very edge of the hangar track where the flood door meets the concrete waterway, with its horizontal grooves and dots of aquatic plant life taking hold. "Now that I have fulfilled my promise," he says, "I will allow you freedom."

He stares at the water above, takes the first step.

I sense something pulling at me. I feel it. Actually *feel* it. Not pulling. Pushing. Falling away. Uncontrolled. Unstoppable. Like wakefulness finally wiping away the last images of a now forgotten dream. The sound fades. The light dims. Shades of black. The inside of eyelids. A starless night. Eternity. Emptiness. Nothing.

Nothing.

5

AND THEN A SINGLE LIGHT.

I feel myself lean back. Shapes begin to appear in the darkness in front of me. I blink—actually blink—and see myself staring. It's dark but clear, the hazel eyes, the round-tipped nose. I flex my jaw and see the muscles highlight instead of shadows under them. Different cause but same effect. I rub one finger over the crescent scar under my eye. I feel the gap of skin with my finger, and the finger on my face.

Shapes emerge from the darkness, reflected in

front of me from behind. Tall bookshelves loaded with thick texts. I step back. The orange uniform remains, the brightness dulled in the tinted reflection. The big, boxy desk comes into sight as I turn. The framed diplomas on the wall behind the desk, the thin computer monitor, more tall shelves loaded with thick books, a door with finger paintings. Burnett's office.

The room appears even sharper here than in any memory. I see the stray drops of paint on the papers behind the door, the titles of the books on the shelves, from the thick ones near the top—*Predicting Teens: Behavioral Therapy and the Adolescent Mind* and *Overcoming Fallacy: How Cognitive Conditioning in Childhood Leads to Happier Adulthood*—to the thin ones on the bottom shelves—*Green Eggs and Ham* and *Cloudy With a Chance of Meatballs*. I see a small ink stain on the couch cushion next to the one I used to sit on, and even the slight hue change where the carpet has moved in different directions. A vivid array of colors on the children's books, board games, and finger paints stands out against the deep black and grays of the psychology books higher on the shelves, and the warm brown of the table, chair, and couch. Even my own orange clothes appear muted in relation. The room feels almost too thick, like an old movie with the color added decades later.

I open the office front door. I step toward the waiting area outside. The metal puzzles remain, as does the couch where I'd sit every week after my session as my parents spoke with Dr. Burnett. There are the same scratches in the table where other kids—or I thought other kids—slid the metal pieces across the lacquer. Everything is exactly as it has always been.

I step back inside the office and see myself in the window again. The reflection of the room is stronger than the darkness outside the window. I reach out for the light switch on the wall. My fingers brush over the subtle bumps, a small drop of dried paint at the top of the light switch cover. I flip the light switch. Nothing happens. I flip on-off, on-off. The lights overhead remain lit.

I hear the rustle of the carpet as I step forward. The doorknob is cold in my fingers as I close the office door behind me. The handle makes a thin metallic click as it turns. I walk across the room and watch the shadows appear as my clothes fold and shift with every movement. At the start of my second session, Burnett asked me not to touch the glass. Its surface is solid and smooth. There is a very subtle vibration from outside. I see the ridges of my finger-prints in the smudge left where I touched the glass. I place my hands against the glass again. I lean in close until all I see are my own eyes reflecting back. Closer. There doesn't seem to be anything outside. The city is gone. The mountains, the people, the cars. Nothing but the thick black I'd seen before. I press forward until I feel the glass pushing against my forehead. Then I move closer.

Shades of black refine into hues of green and brown and gray. Faint shadows suggest upright surfaces of the skyline. A city emerges. Not the city I used to look down on from this window, a city without the immediate congestion of buildings. It's lower and broader, with wide highways looping into narrower roads, large lettering scrawled across bill-boards and flashing signs, cars rushing to stop, and pedestrians striding past each other.

I see myself there. On the sidewalk with three other boys. It's a sunny day, hot enough that other pedestrians are in tank tops and t-shirts. I'm younger, maybe fourteen or fifteen years old, wearing a plain, black sleeveless shirt that I don't recognize, skinny arms hanging out for everyone to see, and loose shorts with giant shoes that make my feet look like robot feet. A baseball cap. I haven't worn one of those in . . . I can't remember when . . . I can't even look back on it. A big silver watch like that of an old man sags heavily on my wrist. I don't recognize any of the other boys. I don't recognize the street or the shops or the buildings. But I know them. I point at one and tell another boy that that's where Joe found twenty bucks lying next to a trash can. The other boy says, "We should go look for some ourselves."

I say, "Someone must've dropped it while throwing their shit away. Not gonna happen again."

The other boy shrugs and says, "It would be awesome to find twenty bucks."

"Better to find a hundred," I say.

I see myself in the window as I withdraw from it, the self that I know now, with the shaved head and the scar and orange uniform that marks me as subject or prisoner. I press closer again. I don't feel the glass this time. The images come more quickly: small, sparse buildings, few cars, and many people. I see snow on the ground and everyone in black overcoats. I'm not there. I know this. I feel this as much as I feel anything. No. I'm elsewhere. Somewhere else.

This is somewhere else. Everything and nothing.

I step back and in again. I see rail cars and Studebakers, wooden frames around unfinished buildings, cities collapsing away into towns and trading posts and little settlements along the edge of a river—centuries rewinding in seconds—settlements becoming untouched wetlands with long-beaked birds digging into the damp dirt.

Wendell must have come from here. He must have watched me through this window. And now here I am. Cut off from my world and thrust into his. If he could enter my window then I should be able to as well. At least I can find him, get back into my head. I can find a way to stop him.

A word enters my mind as though whispered. I move away to look at the window again, from the ceiling to the floor. The reflection of me and the room, the glass between, and the darkness of the other side. The word returns as though written into my thoughts. An energy given form.

"Eden."

That is all.

All that is.

6

IT'S SECOND AND SIX FROM OUR OWN FORTY-FIVE YARD line. Our quarterback yells out a series of false signals. His head jolts forward slightly on every word. The ball snaps on the fourth call. I run diagonally forward, arms open for the handoff. I wrap the ball in one arm and jump to the right. I run as fast as I can, lost behind the big guys up front and easily outpacing the defensive lineman who broke through the block. Around the corner. Another defender rushes toward me. I fake right then left. He wobbles. His feet start to go. I hop right and take off. The ball swings against my chest. There is a blur from the side. I cover the ball before the hit comes. The damn wide receiver missed another block. Third time this game.

One of our linemen grabs my hand and practically deadlifts me off the ground. He slaps my helmet. "Nice," he says. I nod to him while turning to the sideline. First and ten from their forty-seven. I eye out the wide receiver on my way to the sideline. He pretends not to notice.

The next play is a pass in his direction, but the defender knocks the ball out of his hands. Coach yells for me and the other back to head in, pitch play to me on the left side. Won't matter if the receiver misses the block this time.

We ended up losing the game 14-17. I ran for ninety-eight yards and one touchdown, an inside handoff from the seventeen with an excellent block from the fullback, who's twice as I wide as I am, making it easy to simply hide behind him before bursting forward, and with another twenty-three yards receiving. Mom and Dad wait for me at the bottom of the bleachers as I head off the field.

"Not a bad game," Dad says. He has graying temples, small eyes, and his nose has the wide, flat bridge of someone who's been punched a few times. The damage isn't too severe, but enough to be noticeable. His belly is a far more obvious sign of him not not having been an athlete for several years.

"Would've broken a hundred rushing if Jenkins learned to fucking block," I say, looking for the receiver among the rest of the team walking to the locker room.

"Odin!" Mom says, scowling. She's where I got my light-colored eyes from. With the dark skin and hair they give her a striking, exotic look that almost doesn't seem real. Zisa, my eight-year-old sister, stares up at Mom. She inherited dad's eyes.

"Sorry, but it's true." Dad slaps me on the shoulder pad for swearing.

"You riding home with us or heading out?" Mom asks.

"You can go ahead," I say. "Me and Monie are getting some food in a while."

"All right," Mom says. "Call if you'll be home later than eleven."

I nod and start to turn toward the rest of the team. I hear a "hey" from over my shoulder.

Dad leans out over the rail and motions for me to come forward.

"Next time, run right up on that receiver and shove him into the blocker. That'll teach him." He rustles my hair and lightly pushes me away.

Dad works as a security guard for a hospital about five miles from our apartment. He drives there every morning before Zisa and I wake up. Mom works as a lecturer in remedial English for a couple of community colleges around the city, different hours for different days, different days for different semesters. I'm responsible for walking Zisa to and from school every day. She's never been late. Monie, Monica, is my girlfriend. We've been dating for three months. After every game we get some food, usually a burger or something fast. We eat in one of the three open lots around her house and then have sex in the front seat of her used Honda. It feels too awkward to watch. Too voyeuristic. We stay in our reclined seats with the windows fogged until the cops come to tell us we can't sleep there.

"Still thinking about colleges?" Dad asks.

The building cafeteria is almost completely empty. All the other workers have already gone back to their jobs. Every Wednesday, my supervisor, Ms. Sheridan, allows me to take lunch an hour later than normal. That way, Dad and I can be left alone. Ms. Sheridan gives a knowing smile every time I leave for the elevator, as most of the other summer interns are returning to the little cubby office we cycle in and out of. She's also an only child and her parents divorced when she was in high school too. She knows what it's like.

"Yeah," I say, picking out the ham in the sandwich he bought for me before I arrived. "Still waiting to hear from Emory but Georgia and Maryland look good."

"Both good schools," he says. "But I'm sure Emory will work out."

I shrug. "Even if I get in, no idea how to pay for it."

"You'll find a way. I'll of course help however I can."

I continue pulling large slices of meat from between the bread, scraping the bits of lettuce and tomato stuck to it back into the sandwich.

"How's the job? Learning what it's like to be a big time lawyer?"

"I guess so," I say. I don't look at him.

"Look I'm sorry, okay? I didn't remember."

I drop the last slice onto the plate and stare up at him with a look that tells him he's nothing more than an inconvenience, a nuisance in an otherwise pleasant day. That this hour we spend together every week, an hour that Mom encouraged me to take as part of their informal settlement, is the worst of the entire week.

"I've told you every time for the last month."

"Yeah, but after seventeen years, it's hard to remember the sudden change from eating meat."

"Whatever," I say, taking my first bite.

He looks down and away. He's on hostile ground and knows it. Not only with me, but with the entire building. Technically I shouldn't even be here until after high school, but Mom got her new boyfriend to pull some strings. He said I was a bright kid and really interested in international law. Dad looks over to where a pair of cashiers watch a baseball game on the television behind the counter, then to the rows of empty tables extending out from where we are in the corner.

"It's really great you got this chance," he says. "Nice of . . . Alan?"

"Yeah," I say between bites.

"Nice of him to fix you up this way."

"Technically, it wasn't him."

"Still, he talked to his friends who talked to their friends and here you are." He tries to smile. "Moving up in the world, like I always knew you would."

"It's answering phones and making coffee."

"That's the way Starbucks started, too." He gives a cheery, closed-up grin. I just stare back.

After about fifty more minutes of awkward conversation, I tell him it's time for me to return to my non-paying job upstairs.

"Right," he says with a slight sneer, "need to make sure the coffee is ready."

"Whatever," I say, checking to make sure no food got on my tie.

He stands up and walks around the edge of the table to cut me off before I can leave. He puts his arms out for a hug. I lean in and lightly pat his back while he puts both arms around me and squeezes.

"Next week," he says, "I'll remember."

"I'm sure you will," I say half in truth.

Maybe he looks back as we walk away from each other. I don't care.

My friends and I enter the will call box office to claim the tickets we all purchased two weeks ago. It's the first time this group of Shaolin Monks have ever performed outside of China. I became interested in seeing them after watching a clip on YouTube of a man chopping a leafy, green vegetable with a cleaver on his own chest without denting his skin. Then another clip of a little kid putting one leg straight up, his feet at six and twelve o'clock, and falling to the stage in a split. It was the last one that caught my friends' eyes though: two men jumping, spinning, and flipping as they swing swords and spears sharp enough to slice bamboo with a single cut at each other at full speed. "It's amazing what the body is capable of," I wrote when I tagged my friends on a Facebook post with a link to the ticket information, knowing they may not be as interested.

The woman behind the counter in the ticket office looks over each of us. We're easily thirty years younger than anyone else in the line. She stops when she sees me, just over the counter. "Excuse me," she says as she stands and walks through a door in the back of the room.

"Goddammit," says my friend Wesley. We met a year ago when he first transferred to our school a few days after I finally returned. He sighs and thumps his fingers against the countertop. I met my other friend in sixth grade, Gina. She was the only kid in the class who ran faster than I did. She shrugs gently. "Probably just checking the seats."

The ticket lady returns with an older man who

I assume is her boss. He looks at me, leans over the counter and whispers, "I'm sorry, son, it's a very old theater. We don't have wheelchair ramps."

"Such bullshit," says Wesley.

Gina frowns.

"Ever heard of the ADA?" Wesley says to the woman and her boss. Their eyes cast downward.

"I can stay in the back," I say. "I don't mind." After six months in the chair, I've become accustomed to people not being accustomed to me.

Wesley shakes his head. "Fuckers," he mutters.

Gina throws him a look. "No need to be rude, Wes, they're trying."

"They're the ones being rude."

The old man points at something on the computer screen. A seating chart with those sold in red and those open in yellow. I can see it. Not the me in the wheelchair. Not him. Me. The me that's watching me in the wheelchair, on the football field, at lunch with my birth father, winning the state science fair, being arrested for shoplifting or assault or even for murder, sexting with four different girls at once, fighting with my parents, my brothers, my sisters, or any other number of other possible lives. I'm the one that sees it, even if I, the one living that possibility, never do. Even if he, the other Odin, is never aware of his place among the millions of other selves in the universe, I am. They live their lives. Our lives. I'm the one on the outside. The me that sees me being me.

I step away from the window once again. The motion forward and back has become automatic, like a rocking chair, although I sit on the floor. It's gotten easier to find myself in every new world I see. I concentrate on something specific about myself—my face, my voice, a memory that I imagine I'd have, almost anything because that's what's possible—and that life appears before me. The process is similar to the way I viewed the past while in my world, in my own head, only it's different versions of me. There hasn't been any noticeable pattern in how the worlds come up. It's as though my infinite lives are put on shuffle. Every new world plays randomly before me.

The only constant I've found is that in every world, I'm just Odin, although sometimes I have a different name. In no other world is there Wendell or powers. My parents, those who were there when I was born, remain my parents. They may be divorced or remarried. One or both may die in a million ways. I never meet Ben and Aida, or Dr. Burnett, or General Delgado. I never have reason to. I never move across the country. I never meet Evelyn or Brent or Kevin or anyone else. I never even step foot in this office. There may be other worlds like my own, other possibilities, but I have yet to see them. It's the only world I want to see, and I can't find it. It's like looking for one specific needle in a pile of identical needles.

The curious thing is seeing just how little I matter in each of these other worlds. After Burnett's claims that I could save the world with my powers, watching as other worlds continue on fine without me is . . . humbling. Makes me wonder if Wendell saw these things when he was here. Is that why he chose my world?

There are worlds, thousands of them, where I was never born. I feel those immediately. Not having a natural vantage point makes these worlds harder to view. There are other thousands of worlds where I die as a baby, a child, a teenager, from car crashes, hit-and-runs, leukemia, the flu, and one world where I forgot to tighten my containment suit before leaving the shelter for school, contracted radiation poisoning, and died five minutes later. I've seen myself stabbed on my way to a bookstore, jump off my apartment balcony after my first girlfriend dumped me, shot by my mother when using the fire escape to enter the apartment because I forgot my key, shot while knocking on a neighbor's door to give them misfiled mail, shot for looking suspicious while walking through a different neighborhood after dark. Among the millions of possible ways to die, it's a wonder there are enough worlds in which I live this long.

I've seen my parents mourn and cry, sometimes for years, sometimes splitting up in grief, dividing my siblings among themselves. Sometimes they quietly move on with their lives, replacing me in their minds and hearts within a matter of months or weeks. My friends, the ones I, this I, have never known, always recover much more quickly.

There are Ben and Aida, even Andre, in the same house where I lived in my world. Without me, Ben is never moved into Project Solar Flare. He leaves government service and becomes a physical therapist for people recovering from traumatic injuries. Aida takes law classes at night, leaving Andre with his father. She chides Ben for spoiling their son too much, making him chubby with too many desserts on nights when they're left alone in the house. He jokes that he can't help it, he sees people struggle every day and wants at least one person to be happy when he's around. They never speak to Dr. Burnett in this world. They never know me. They never have to hide or lie about who they are. They never worry about being caught or some catastrophe occurring. They never allow a potential monster into their lives.

Kevin enters high school as an awkward kid who didn't have many friends in middle school. He's made fun of by T.J. for being too much of a loner. Kevin and Brent bond over video games and mutual annoyance by the assholes who want to pick on others. He's a good guy in this world too, Brent, still reaches out to outcasts and popular kids alike. He and Kevin talk about Evelyn, the pretty girl they've seen while rounding the field during baseball practice. She and Brent never hang out or talk outside of a couple of short interactions during class. "Hey, can I borrow a pencil?"

Her sigh, "Sure," tells him she's not interested. Richard asks her out but she says no. That's life without me, one of them, there are infinite variations.

I've seen a world where Brent's family moves to Japan when he's ten. One where Evelyn breaks her ankle in the first track meet of the year, gains a lot of weight, and takes depression out by cutting herself. Another where Kevin enters a different high school and starts a punk band that becomes legendary for playing their song "Fuck Mr. Parkman" (the math teacher everyone hates) during an assembly, and hundreds of others. Never in any world do they meet me. I guess, in a way, I really am unique in the whole of eternity. And, pulling back from a world in which Ben and Aida decided to move to Naples after taking a vacation there, I know that I am so infinitely tiny. One in billions of parts in one of billions of worlds. Not even a drop in the ocean. A single electron in a single atom in a single molecule in a single drop in the ocean. That is how truly unimportant I am to any world but my own, the one world that I just can't fucking find. I even tried keying in on the scar over my orbital bone. There are hundreds of worlds where I have that too.

I stare at my reflection in the window. The me I know. A freak of probability. An invisible observer. I am what Wendell was. Displaced. Trying, more than anything, trying, to find home. Not that it matters. No matter. No matter at all.

The words enter my mind as they did before. Formless yet solid, almost tangible, as though directly connected into my being. "Don't be sad." It's a vibration given shape. "You are welcome here."

7

I STAND AND TURN TOWARD THE REST OF THE OFFICE. The couch I remember sitting on, the chair where Burnett would lean to one side with one arm extended and the other resting and pointed directly at me. The finger paintings on the door with the artist's name scribbled in the corner.

The vibration continues. "Focus," it says. "Think of something to attach me to."

The sound in my head is soft and smooth, high and gentle, like a young girl's voice. She's maybe nine or ten years old, with big, brown eyes and a little curved nose and round baby cheeks, the way Evelyn must have looked when she was young, but with ears that stick out slightly like an elf. That's how she appears in the room in front of me.

She looks over each of the walls, eyes wide but shallow, as if painted on. She stares into every corner. She leans to read the names off the game boxes in the open cabinet near the couch. She even seems to admire the titles of the psychology books on the shelf. She turns to me last.

"Good," she says, looking up. She wears a plaid dress over a white turtle-neck sweater. I'm still in my orange uniform. "What's your name?" she asks.

"Ummm," I say. It takes half a moment to remember how to actually speak. "Odin."

"I'm Eden. Nice to finally meet you." She stares up with a closed-mouth smile that presses her cheeks outward.

"What is this place?" I ask. The echo in my throat makes my voice exactly as I'd always heard it.

She glances around quickly. "I think someplace from your memory."

"I mean where in the world . . . or in the universe is this room?"

She appears puzzled for a second. "We're not really anywhere in the universe. We're outside of it. Outside with everything else inside."

"You live here too?"

"No." She shakes her head. "I am here."

"So . . . I'm imagining you?"

She continues to stare up at me. It's almost unsettling the way she never blinks or breathes. "Kind of, but not quite. It is just easiest to communicate with you this way." She smiles again, showing two big front teeth. "It's best to start with something familiar and build from there."

"Build?"

"Yeah. Anything you want."

"Are you here alone?" I ask.

She looks puzzled again, as though searching for something with which to reference this word. "Alone?"

"Is anyone else here?"

"Everything is here," she says sweetly, almost whimsical in her tone.

"Anyone else like me. Anyone . . . ummm . . . real?"

She shakes her head with such force it looks like she might fall over. "You're the only person here. The only," she pauses searching for the word, "intelligence."

"Ever?" Wendell must have been here; it's where he came from.

"Yes."

I furrow my brow. "How is that possible?"

"Umm." She looks away. "I don't know how to answer that."

"There wasn't someone here just a little while ago? Someone exactly like me?"

She frowns and shakes her head. It looks as though I've scolded her. How could she not have any knowledge of Wendell? He must have been here before me.

"What is 'a little while'?" she asks.

"A short time, like an hour."

She stares.

"Do you know what 'hour' means?"

"I know the word and what it means but not how long it is."

"Because you don't have time here," I say.

She shrugs.

"So does that mean time is frozen? Or is it speeding ahead like with space travel?"

"Ummm . . . yes?"

"You have no idea what I mean, do you?" I say.

"No." She looks away shyly. "I never had to."

Even if I manage to find my world and return to it, will it be too late to stop Wendell from tearing the planet apart, or will it be only seconds after his escape? Could I even go backwards and stop him from ever entering my mind in the first place?

I look down at her, her eyes big and unblinking as ever. Without some concept of years, days, minutes, how would Eden understand what I'm asking? Better to find out for myself.

"How can I see my world?" I ask.

"All of these worlds are yours," she says, as though I should have learned this long ago. "Every life is happening now. Everything before now is done. Everything after now is . . . not done."

"You mean the future is unknown."

She considers what to say. "I mean . . . for me there is only ever now. The past is set. It never changes. And the future . . . " She tilts her head in thought. " . . . is . . . " She straightens out. " . . . always being made now."

I lean against the window behind me. "You don't know which one of these is the world where I actually come from?"

She shakes her head.

"You can't help me find it?"

"I'm sorry," she says, her whole body sags.

"What about those worlds in which I've died

or was never born?" I ask. "I've seen hundreds of them. That's not my existence."

"Those worlds are still possibilities of life. You may not be in them but that doesn't mean they don't continue without you, on their own."

"I've noticed," I mutter. Seems that way for every world.

I feel the glass against my back. I'd probably never stand this way in the real world. Not because of the smudging, but because there's some part of me that's afraid the glass would shatter and I'd fall through. I know the likelihood of that happening is extremely low, but there's still a possibility. Perhaps even some other world where such a thing happens. All these different lives I could have had. The good ones, the bad ones— huge changes for me; no change for the rest of the world. I sigh.

"That doesn't mean you shouldn't look," she says with a perk in her voice.

"I have. I don't even know where to begin."

"Hmmm . . . maybe you could look somewhere else?"

"How?"

"This place," she says, looking around the room again, "it comes from your memory. What do you remember outside of it?"

"Outside?"

"Yeah. Through that window. What did you see there?"

"Buildings, people on the road, cars, street lights, all the normal things."

"Think of something specific. Something that it feels like you could grab onto."

I try to remember. It's been years since the last time I'd been in Burnett's office. Burnett's real office. It's much harder to be clear about that time without being able to look back directly on it. If I could still do that, I wouldn't be searching for my world in the first place. I close my eyes to help the memory.

"There's one building across the street from

here. It's about half as tall as this one. There's a garden on the roof that looks like no one has visited in years." The more I speak the clearer the memory becomes. "All the pots are filled with piles of dirt along each side of the roof, with the door to the staircase kind of off the center. There's a hose rolled up next to the door to the roof. I never saw anyone go there. There are a lot of birds though, pecking at the dirt piles." I hear birds chirping. Sounds of wind and traffic below. I open my eyes.

Eden and I stand on the rooftop. It isn't exactly as I described it. It's so much more. The gray pots have cracks and weather wear on them. The handle for the hose is brittle from rust. Over the walls, the city spreads out around us. Engine noises, car horns, and a distant siren all fill the air. There's even a smell of mold, old bird shit, and car exhaust, all things I'd hated before but now they feel like vital parts of life. The suburbs roll out far beyond the city. Then the mountains to the very edge of my vision.

"What is this?" I ask.

"This is outside of the room. How you remember it."

Burnett's building stretches far above us. A structure of blinding glass windows that don't seem to ever end. "How did we get here?"

"You made it. You can make anything here. You can even change things if you don't like them."

I must look confused because she motions for me to follow her to one of the neglected plant pots. There are old cigarette butts and chewed gum dropped in the dirt.

"Start with something small," she says. "Just, imagine it's there."

A blade of grass, bright green, almost yellow, sprouts from the dirt in the pot.

"Good start," Eden says.

"How will this help me find my world?" She shrugs. "Maybe learning more about this one."

She nods. "I think that will help."

More grass fills in the empty pot. The cigarette

butts and gum disappear from sight. Next, maybe a flower or two, little yellow and white ones popping randomly from the grass. Or, they could be the pinkish orange blossoms like those the neighbors across the street planted when they moved in last year. Why not blue or red, or even black, black with a yellow center and blue specks along the petals and the . . . what's the thing in the middle? I don't know. I can't find it.

"That's very pretty," she says. Of the bursting arrangement of pedals and colors that have sprung up where there was empty dirt before.

"Never been much of a flower guy, but I guess it's all right," I say.

"I've never seen flowers before."

"In that case these are the best flowers ever."

She laughs, a gentle little kid laugh that's probably too generous for what was said. "Is this what your world is like?"

"Parts of it," I say, moving from the pot to the edge of the roof. "Very small parts."

"You can make more if you want," she says, an eagerness to her voice, as though she hopes to see what else comes out of my imagination. "What would you most like to see right now?"

"I'd like to see what's happened to my world. I want to know that the people are safe there. But I can't find it."

"Just because you can't find their world doesn't mean you can't see them," she says.

"That's not the same."

"Why not?"

"Because it won't really be them." I look to the building across the street. I squint my eyes as the sun reflects off the glass. I can see other people passing by windows into other offices. Burnett's was on the 25th floor, near the left corner but not on the corner. The sun blocks that floor and several above and below from my vision.

"If you know them, then they will be real," Eden says.

I turn to see her staring, eyes almost excessively

large, cheeks blank and little mouth in a tight pout.

"They can at least keep you company while you look," she says after a moment. "Maybe having them around will help you find your world more easily."

"It's not the same. They won't be them. They'll be my version of them."

"I'm sure they'd be happy just to have you again, Odin."

Aida would push right up and hug me. She'd kiss my cheek and say that she was sorry for ever doubting my place in their family and that I truly was their son, always have been and always will be. She'd let go long enough for Ben to step forward, crack some faux unimpressed smile and say that springing grass and flowers out of dirt is almost as cool as that time he found a completely untouched box of donuts sitting on top of a mailbox, and not just the cheap glazed kind, the deluxe assorted kind. He'd put out his hand to shake, and when I'd reach for it, he'd grab me into a hug, slapping my back so hard I'd almost cough. Andre would ask where I've been. I'd look at Ben and Aida, both of them silent, leaving it to me to decide how to respond. "Away," I'd say. "Somewhere else."

"Was it fun?" he'd ask.

"Sometimes."

"Cool," he'd say. Then, "You should have seen what Alvin did the other day during math class." Aida would tell him that the stories can wait. We have a lot of catching up to do.

I actually feel her hand on my head now, rubbing on the stubble left since my last shave. It's odd that I'd still imagine myself that way. "Did you do that?" she asks.

"Not by choice," I say. She steps back to look at me, hand on my shoulder. The bit of water at the corner of her eyes reflects the light off the sun above us.

They're here.

They're really here.

Our house has grown around us. The gray couch that replaced the old one. The off-white carpeting that ends at the dining room and kitchen tile. The photograph in the hand-carved wooden frame next to the television. We posed for the shot three years ago at Trout Beach after spending the day riding bikes in the park.

"It looks good," Aida says, lightly running one finger over my head. "Very hip."

"I doubt that's the look they were going for," I say.

"Very round," Ben adds. "At least this way you know that if you ever go bald, your head won't look too weird."

Aida hugs my shoulders and rests her head against mine. "It's good to have you back," she says, trying her best to cover the sniffles. "I'm sorry," she whispers.

"It's okay," I reply. And it really is. It doesn't matter anymore.

She wipes her face as she steps in front of me. She places both of her hands on my cheeks. I can feel the dampness on them. Ben walks up to just behind her. "We're very proud of you," he says.

I nod. "I know."

"Hey, Odin," hollers Andre from only a few feet away. "Does this mean you're back?"

"I guess so."

"Cool," he says, trying to act like he doesn't care anymore, even though I know he does.

"So," Dad says, as Mom steps away. "Anything new?"

"Ummm . . . "

"Kidding. I'm sure there's absolutely nothing new at all. Just the same old stuff every day."

Mom gives me an irritated look at this. She leans in but doesn't whisper. "I swear he was even worse while you were gone. Like if he made enough bad jokes he suddenly wouldn't be sad."

"I heard that," Dad says. "And I don't make

bad jokes because I'm sad. I make awesome jokes because I'm sad."

She rolls her eyes and looks at me again in way that says, "See? This is what I mean."

"Anyway," she says, sweetly and evenly, "welcome home."

8

"**Y**OU DID ALL THIS?"

Brent indicates the neighborhood around us. Storefronts, cars, pedestrians, street signs and stop lights clutter the gaps and spaces, the little details that we seldom notice but without which our lives wouldn't be as rich.

"Kind of," I say.

We pass a convenience store. Through the door I can see a bored cashier leaning on her fist between racks of impulse buys: candy bars and tabloids with scandalous headlines about some celebrity I've never heard of. A kid with a skateboard sits at a bus stop with an ad for a real estate agent on it. Someone has spray-painted "douche" over the agent's face. I don't recognize either the agent or the kid.

"What's that mean, 'kind of'? There was nothing here before and then there is. That means you built it."

"I don't know that there was nothing here before."

A motorcyclist moves to the front of the cars waiting at the red light. The bike's license plate reads, "HOLDON."

"I didn't specifically imagine most of this either," I say as the light turns and we cross the street. HOLDON speeds off down the road. "None of these cars or people. Not even most of these buildings. They just seemed to pop up out of nothing."

"That's pretty awesome though, man. Wish I could do things like that." His head turns to follow a girl who walks between us in a pair of yoga pants and a tank top with a rolled-up mat under her arms. "Really wish I could."

"Yeah," I say. The green of the traffic lights is more concentrated than any I'd ever seen before. The stores don't have any of the grime they typically do. The only piece of graffiti I can remember is the "douche" over the real estate agent's face. The sky above the stores and in the distance is a vivid, cloudless blue and isn't at all faded by the bright sun. The sun does not feel hot, not even in the black t-shirt that's replaced my orange prison uniform. "Maybe it's like dreaming," I continue, "how there's so much more detail in the dream than you'd normally think. A subconscious kind of thing."

"Maybe," he says. "But who cares? It's awesome." Even he looks a bit different. It could be that the crook in his nose is fixed. I'm not sure.

We stop at the next corner. Across the street is the sandwich shop that used to be a printing center where Mom would get fundraiser fliers made before she invested in her equipment to work from home. Four stores down is the bank that closed about ten years ago and hasn't had anything in it since. Some of the elementary school kids used to practice bicycle tricks in the parking lot. I haven't actually been in this neighborhood for years, yet here it all is, sharper and brighter than ever before.

"So what else is there to do?" Brent asks. "Got any games or anything?"

"Wasn't there, like, an arcade on Seventy-first and Walters?" He shrugs. "I haven't tried making anything like that."

"Why not?" We take the next turn and continue toward the bike shop where Kevin and I used to go in middle school just to look at the new bikes. They had a racing helmet there that I always wanted but never got. I don't even know where we're going right now. I just wanted to go.

"If this were me," he says, "I'd make the whole world into like the best fucking game ever. Sniper perches and exploding cars and all that shit."

"Think I've had enough machine guns for a while," I say.

"All right, then like a fantasy game or something. A jungle with tigers that you make into a pet or a mount. Then when I get sick of it, I'd wipe it all away and start again. Make it whatever I want."

"Maybe I'm just not that imaginative."

"Ha!" he says. "That does beg the big question though, other than where exactly we're going—"

I shrug. After so long of being stuck in one place—the base, the school, the house—moving felt right. It's like being an explorer.

"Why am *I* here?"

"You're still my friend, man." Even the mountains far from the town are visible. "I mean, it was shitty setting me up with those guys, but you had your reasons. I can't just forget about everything else because of that."

"No, no, no, I mean why isn't someone else here instead of me?"

"I figured you meant that. Think I'm just a bit scared to try with her. Maybe she, or maybe my version of her, won't be right. Or maybe she'll act differently. Like subconscious rejection or something." I feel as though I should be able to find a specific term for this idea, but I can't.

"I get that."

"Like, if this were Richard's world, he'd make Maria with really detailed tits and nothing else."

He laughs, "Oh, yeah, like, she'd have no face."

"Evelyn's different though. I mean, she's cute, obviously, but there's that little . . . I dunno, fire I guess. It's hard to describe. She's, like, not too much of anything." I stop to think, staring at nothing. "The way she smiles with one side of her mouth, and her squirrel cheeks, like she knows something you don't and she wants you to know but she won't tell you. Things like that, you know?"

"The imperfections," I hear Brent say.

"Yeah. Imperfections."

Evelyn's voice floats into my mind. "You mean I'm not perfect?"

"No one is," I say, "I mean, no real person."

I look up to see her there, head tilted, long hair pushed back behind her ear, a light overhead bouncing off the diamond on the tip of her nose. Her eyes are dark, as though nothing could ever escape them.

I'm sitting against the bed in my room. She's walked right through the open door. "That's part of the fun though, getting to see who someone is beyond the act they put on for everyone else." She gestures to the floor in front of me. "Do you mind?"

I motion for her to sit. She presses her skirt to the back of her legs as she lowers down. She sits with her feet pointed to one side, knees together, hand propped straight for balance. Spiderman jumps from the wall behind and above her head. "How have you been?" she says, with her eyes up and a little, puff-cheeked smile.

"I'm still trying to figure that out," I say.

"Maybe I can help with that. Are you sad?" Her eyebrows rise.

"A bit," I say.

"But not much?"

"Not particularly."

"Scared?"

"Not anymore."

"Angry?"

I glance up at my bedroom ceiling. The little spot of dirt I never figured out the cause of is gone. I glance down to my hands. The scars from Hauser's window are gone from them as well.

"No. Not right now," I say.

"Hmmm . . . are you at least a little bit happy?"

"Happier, I guess. At least I'm not being followed everywhere I go and manipulated into building a weapon anymore."

"Yeah," she says, nodding, "that would suck." She shifts around, folding her legs under her. She reaches one hand toward my head. "May I? Or would that be weird?"

I lean out. Her hand is warm and smooth,

patting very lightly. I don't recall her ever patting someone's head before.

"It's scratchy," she says.

"Not to me."

She nods. "I like it. Aerodynamic. Probably good for running."

"Thinking of changing your look for extra speed?"

"I doubt my head is quite as round," she says, she crinkles her nose in complete symmetry, as though the two sides were mirrored.

"It's imperfect."

"It is."

I laugh.

"There," she says, "you're a little bit happy."

I stretch my back before looking into yet another world. The city comes into view through the window, as though leaving this room completed the rest of the world around it. The tiny streets are smaller and denser with activity than they were when they first appeared. The rooftops teem with metal shacks, bicycle repair stations, weight benches, so many more personal touches than I'd ever noticed. Roads and houses extend farther into the distance. At the end of my sight, the mountains seem taller than they had been. Low clouds get caught among the peaks. I don't remember if that's ever happened before. Not that it matters.

So far during this trip to the office I've been an honor roll student at a private school, a dropout, a stoner, a bully, a rich kid, and there was even one world where I was blind and looking through my own eyes was nothing but light and dark. It's gotten easier to determine if a world could be mine, other than assuming that none of them are, to find where I am and what I'm doing in the present. It's like locating a television show by watching only seconds to see if it's a new episode or an old one.

"Haven't found it?" I hear the childish voice behind me. I turn to see Eden there, high-necked sweater and plaid dress exactly as before.

"There are just so many."

"What would you do if you found it?"

"Try to find a way back, I guess."

"Do you know how?" She gives that inquisitive look that children have. The look I'm sure I gave Dr. Burnett or my parents many times, although I can't know because I can't see myself in those moments. Not anymore.

"Find a way to push into my mind and somehow take control. It's how the other guy did it." She frowns. "Another version of me. Or maybe I'm another version of him. Either way, he was here but now he's there."

"But you're the only one who's been here."

"I guess so," I say, "I mean, we're technically the same person, just from different worlds."

"How did he get there from here?"

"I let him." She looks both confused and sad.

"I was trapped in a bad place doing something I didn't want to do and he convinced me that the only way out was to let him have control of my mind and body. He could do things I couldn't." It sounded foolish when described out loud, how I was so easily duped by Wendell into giving him the control he'd wanted from the first day we met. But in that moment, staring General Delgado and his troops in the face, it was the only choice. I remember that it was my only choice.

"Sounds like you didn't want to be there," she says.

"I was a prisoner. They told me I was helping people but I was actually helping to make some kind of weapon. He, the other me, said he could destroy the weapon and help me escape. He destroyed the weapon and then he sent me here."

"That's what you wanted?"

"I don't . . . think so." The rooftop garden

across the street is lush with greenery. Even the concrete floor has become a healthy lawn of grass. The streets below are barely visible as more than lines on a map. People are tiny dots. I see the wisp of clouds below me. Never realized just how high up this office is. Maybe because I was shorter when I used to come here.

"Is it like this for everyone?" I ask.

"What do you mean?"

"This place, these possibilities. Is this for everyone or just for all the versions of me?" She shakes her head. "You have no way of knowing," I say.

"How would I?"

I place my hands on the glass and lean in expecting to see another new possibility.

"You let him in," Eden calls out from behind me.

I stop.

"You said it was your choice to give him control."

"It's what I had to do."

"What was happening?"

"I was a prisoner . . . somewhere. They were making me build a weapon for them."

"Who were they?"

"Military, I think. People who wanted to build a weapon. That's weird, I used to be able to see everything from my past perfectly. But since I got here, it's become harder to see it."

"Were you scared?"

"I . . . think so. I mean, of course."

"Yeah," she says, sitting on the carpet next to me. She hugs her knees to her chest. She looks so small there. "Where you were was so horrible that you did whatever you could to escape."

"I had to."

"Can this other version of you make the whole world the way he wants like you can?"

"I don't think so. I mean, it's different in the real world. There are rules and stuff. Not like here."

"Hmmm," she says, as though making a show of thinking. "Doesn't sound to me like your world was a particularly good one. You could probably find something better."

"That's . . . not really the point. I know that he's dangerous and I should stop him."

"Is he always you?"

"No." I know what she's asking. She wants to know if this other me exists in any world other than my own or if he's one possibility within infinity. Even if horrible things were to happen in my world, there will still be other versions of my friends and family. Infinite possibilities stemming from where they are now. Infinite potential. Somewhere in those worlds is one where Evelyn grows up to be an Oscar-winning movie star, where Brent designs the greatest video game ever, where Ben and Aida live a peaceful, simple life and raise Andre without complications. There will always be a better version of me. Even if I never find it. Even if I'm never him.

I see the tree-lined streets below branching ever outward. Clouds like cotton balls floating in the sky. Mountains stretching so high it looks like they're kissing the sun. The world is so big, yet I can see it all. Perfectly clear. Not a bit of it wasted.

"I hope you find your world again, Odin," Eden says, "if that's what will make you happy."

"I think it will." I nod, but I don't know anymore.

9

I STARE OVER THE CROWD SPREADING OUTWARD FROM the second floor railing. The people shuffle between the different shops, carrying big bags with bright logos in one hand and talking to their friends or on cell phones as they walk. I have no idea who any of these people are, where they came from, what makes them appear, but I like seeing them move through the space. I turn and lean my back against the railing, watching the rest of my group.

We're next to the elevator outside the Panorama in the big mall. It's so big I don't even see the exits from here. We're in a circle: me, Evelyn, Maria, Richard, Brent, Kevin. Kevin points at the

Cajun food place in the food court, wondering if you can get drunk off Bourbon chicken if you eat enough of it. Brent says the alcohol burns out in cooking. Kevin knows, he's just saying. He has no scars or lingering marks. His face was never broken. Actually his face looks a bit shorter than I remember and he doesn't wear glasses anymore. Brent points out the Korean barbecue place and says it's good, but a bit too spicy for him.

Maria acts shocked at something Richard said. She rolls her eyes and turns her head. "It was a joke," he says, "I'm totally kidding."

She turns her back on him completely, pretending to shut him out.

"Brent," he says, "please tell Maria I was just kidding."

"I have no idea what he said," Brent says, leaning in slightly to enter their conversation, "but I can tell you for absolute certain that he was totally not kidding."

Maria whips around to point at Brent.

"Thanks, asshole."

"Anytime," says Brent as Kevin stifles a laugh.

The food court seems to span a mile behind them with every type of cuisine imaginable.

"See, even he knows it," Maria says, still pretending to be upset about whatever it was Richard said in the first place. I don't know. I wasn't listening.

"That's cuz he's an asshole," Richard replies.

"Brent? No way, everyone knows Brent is, like, the nicest guy ever."

"It's true, I am," Brent says, again leaning into their conversation.

"He's almost as big of an ass as yours is." Maria's mouth gapes open and she gives Richard the finger. "Is that your favorite finger?" he asks. She nods confidently. "Is that why it smells funny?" Brent and Kevin crack up laughing.

"Oh my god!" she says, mouth dropping open. "You are such an asshole!"

"What?" he says. "I was totally joking." Brent and Kevin continue laughing.

"Hey." I feel the air of the words my ear. Evelyn places her elbows on the railing. "You're being quiet," she says softly, head resting on her shoulder. A cartoonish skull with a yellow crack keeps her hair pinned behind her ears.

I nod.

"What are you thinking about?"

"Nothing."

She smiles. "You've never thought about nothing in your entire life. So either you're experiencing something entirely new, or you don't want to tell me." I shrug. "And in that case I want to know it even more."

I laugh lightly, lips ticking up, and face her. She stares at me with a crooked grin, that evil-cute look that says she'd be willing to torture me and I'd love every second of it. The soft mall lights appear to bounce off her eyes, reflect in the diamond tip of her nose. The only shadows on her face are the light ones from her cheekbones. No other stray marks or blemishes appear.

I glance over to the others. Maria eyes Richard like she's about to punch him in the face and then kiss the wound. Brent and Kevin watch as a pair of college-age girls in tight jeans walk by.

"Just that it's nice to be here," I say. "Having everyone around like this."

She tilts her head, hair swinging like ripples in a pond after a light wind, the sly grin replaced by kindness. "Where else would we be?" she asks.

"I dunno. Not here. Somewhere else, I suppose."

"Hmmm . . . " she says, pursing her lips. She looks almost angular that way. "Kind of disappointing."

"What?"

"I thought you'd be thinking about types of existential being or something." She smirks. "Get it? Thinking about nothing?" I shake my head, feeling a big, cheesy grin plastered on my face. "C'mon, you know you liked that."

"That was awful," I say with a laugh.

"Made you laugh, though." Her look is one of

confident challenge, knowing that she could say anything and I'd love all of it. She glances over her shoulder before leaning her head the tiniest bit closer to mine. "You wanna go up the hill later tonight?" she whispers. Her breath is lilac.

"Anytime," I say.

"Good."

I feel the entire railing move, bouncing my back off the wall.

"Evie," Maria says, tossing her head back so her hair flops down heavily. "They're being total dicks to me." Evelyn looks up at me and sighs. "Tell them to stop," Maria whines.

"It was a joke," says Kevin.

"Yeah," says Brent, "we're totally kidding."

I hear loud laughter from below me. Among the crowd is a woman raising her brows as she speaks to a man with sharp features. He nods and laughs with her.

It all looks so small from here, the skyline melting into stars. A canopy overhead while its duplicate stretches across the land. A seamless transition from city to sky, and then up higher where entire galaxies swirl in an outwardly chaotic balance. There appear to be more stars than there is space between them. Yet down here, on the little hill Evelyn and I sit on to watch the city lights blend into the night sky, it's still and silent and dark.

"It's amazing to think there's still so much out there," Evelyn says, leaning back and looking up.

"More than anyone can imagine," I say.

"Even you?" she says with a quick glance. Her dark eyes seem to consume all light.

"Especially me."

We sit on the blanket I placed on the grass because it felt more authentic that way, the kind of place I imagine people would go to be alone with the guarantee that absolutely no one else will find them. This is just for us.

She sits with her legs stretched out, arms locked back to hold her up, staring into forever.

"I bet you could." Her hair is one long, black shadow stretching to her back. "You could probably create whole new worlds if you wanted. Fill the galaxy with unbelievable things."

I lay back on my elbows staring up the way she does.

"I honestly never thought that much beyond my own life."

"Me neither," she says. "But then you see something like this and it makes you wonder." She adjusts to sit up, drawing her legs under her. She continues staring at the stars. I sit up as well. "Wonder if it just goes on and on," she says, "until it ends."

The light rides the contours of her face, the soft curves of her cheeks and forehead, a smooth layer over gentle slopes, until it too disappears completely, hiding where she ends and the darkness begins.

"We don't know that," I say. "Maybe there's still more."

She chuckles. "I didn't mean that in a sad way, Odin." She looks down at her hands, rubbing her palms together. "It just makes me think of how amazing it is that something like this exists and that we get to see it. It makes me think of how remarkably insignificant and yet wholly unique and important we are. As tiny as we may be, without us, there's no one else to enjoy it all."

I see the shadows in her eyes turn to me.

"Sorry," she says, "I'm being weird again."

I shake my head. "Not weird," I say. "You're right. Guess I'm just used to being contained, you know? School, parents, do this, do that, be here at this time for this long then go there." I survey the scenery from one horizon to the other. "It's nice to see something that's so . . . limitless."

I feel a weight on my shoulder. I hear the rustle of her hair. She glows.

"Thank you," she says as a single breath.

I lean my head lightly on hers. "What for?" I whisper.

She peeks up, half of her face lit and one speck of light bouncing from one eye. "For bringing me here. For choosing me to share this with."

"I can't imagine anyone I'd rather have with me."

She presses her lips against mine. They're warm and damp and soft and she smells like lavender. I feel every bit of this. I know I do.

I hear the smooth slide of fabric running together. I feel the light brush of her hands across my shoulders and chest, her weight on my legs. She's a silhouette in front of me, blocking out the world behind her. She is everything.

"Is this okay?" she says, bouncing just slightly on my lap. "Not too much?"

I shake my head. "Perfect."

Her hand runs down my arm. Every nerve in my body swarms to the little fingers tracing my skin and wrapping around my wrist. I feel the weight of my arm lifting, then a warmth in my palm. Soft and firm and smooth and bare and curving perfectly, just as I imagined. She kisses me again, harder this time, pressing my head back as her arms pull me in. I knew she would do that. Knew this would happen here, now. It is exactly as I hoped.

I knew it all. Everything that's going to happen. How it's supposed to feel. Like it's been practiced.

I see Evelyn there that morning in the library. She leaned toward me across the table. The lights overhead and off the table dove into her eyes like a hallway, cast small craters into the shallow marks on one round cheek, brought out the redness of the skin under her hairline. She looked down at the silver heart and skull charms on her bracelet. She said she'd never be able to experience what it's like to be Bianca. She's knows everything that's going to happen to her but she, Bianca, does not. For Bianca it's real. For Evelyn and for me it's an act. We already know this play.

"Wait," I say.

I place my hands on her shoulders to hold her away. At least I think I do.

"What's wrong?"

I try to push back from her weight. She's an outline in front of me. An empty shadow with a world outside of her.

"I thought this is what you wanted."

"It is. Just . . . not like this." There's still the press of her weight, the lavender smell, the warmth of her breath. I can still feel the heat of her skin lingering in my palm. She's still there, blocking out everything else. A hollow shape and nothing more. "Not like this," I say again.

"Why?" Her fingers pass lightly across my chin. She whispers, "Don't you want me?"

"This . . . isn't real."

"It is real." She slides up my legs. "As real as anything else."

"It's not. It's an act."

"So is everything," she says. "Everything that

you think is real. Every feeling you have, every memory and sensation and desire is a function of your mind. So this," she kisses me again, her lips are still soft and warm and wet, "this is as real as anything else you've ever felt."

"No," I say, no longer squirming or holding her back. Sitting stoic instead. "And it never will be."

I feel her weight shift. She leans back until her face catches the light like a blanket thrown over her. Streaks of hair drape over slim shoulders, darkness at the center of her eyes.

"Am I not good enough for you?" she says. "Am I not giving you everything you ever wanted?"

"That's it," I say, hearing a quiver in my voice. "It's too much. It's too . . . perfect."

"What's wrong with that? Why can't things be perfect? Isn't that better than tragedy and horror and chaos? Isn't that what you came here for? To escape?"

"But it's not real."

"Odin, don't you deserve the best life possible?

Why shouldn't you have everything you can imagine?"

"That's life," I say. "That's *real* life. As clichéd as it is."

"No, *this* is real. This," she squeezes my wrist and holds my hand firm against her breast, "is what you've always wanted."

I shake my head. "No," I mutter. "You're ruining it. She's not like this."

"Anything you want, Odin, you can have it all."

The pressure lessens on my wrist. Her skin fades from my palms.

"Not real," I say.

"I can do anything for you."

I feel her weight begin to lift. The smell and the warmth dissipate.

"Please," she says, "I can make you happy." Her voice begins to vanish. "Don't push me away. Don't . . . " The layer of light over her fades. "Don't leave me here alone . . . "

Darkness. Complete and absolute. I see the

ridges of my fingerprints on the glass, my reflection staring back, sunken and tired. The office appears behind me in the window. I run my hand over the carpet as I turn; no color change follows the contact. The chair and couch are a drab brown. The thick books on the upper shelves are blank and those near the bottom are empty colors. Finger paintings remain on the door but I can't tell what they are. No names appear on the paper. The wall behind the desk has a few frames. The papers contained are blurs. The desk is empty except for a computer screen and a pen in a stand. In the cabinet on the other side of the room there are checkers, chess, playing cards, board games. I see a stack of colored boxes covered with large letters. On top of the boxes are metal shapes with rings attached. This is exactly as I remember this office—Burnett's office. Nothing less and absolutely nothing more. I turn back to the completely and absolutely dark window.

Somewhere in that window is my world. The

one with the people I know and care about. Evelyn—the real Evelyn—Ben and Aida, Andre, Brent, Dr. Burnett, even, apparently, Kevin, Richard, and Maria. Everyone. Derek and the baseball players, Evan and the other gamers, Alison and the Drama Club girls, Teddy and the guys from the lunch table, Terri from the girls' bowling team, Jenny Robinson, Tyler and the seniors, Dylan, Eric, Ross and T.J., David the traitor, the people I barely know, the people I've never met and never will but who still live as much as anyone else, Randall Choi, Edward Delgado, Rogers and McPhers—No. He's gone. The crack of McPherson's neck rings as a sharp snap through every cavern in my mind. All these people living the only lives they've ever known, as precious to them as anything else in all of creation. Without it there is nothing else.

That's what Burnett and my parents and Choi wanted me to learn. Power, the power I had, is measured in relation to how it affects the others around you. There is no power in isolation, not good, not bad, just . . . nothing. What's the point in being unique, if you can't share it with anyone else? And what's the point of being powerful if it doesn't make life better? There are already so many chances at pain and sadness and misery, so many possibilities for tragedy, why provide more?

That's why they—Burnett, Choi, Ben, Aida, Solar Flare, all of them—chose to shelter me and condition me. That's why they wanted to control me. They knew what power is.

Now I do too.

I also know that you can't control power. No matter how much you may try, there will always be someone, something, pulling it away, twisting it, manipulating it for themselves and their use, for their own betterment. They want it just to have it, just to do what they please. But I know better. I was raised better than that.

Power, life, they're not about controlling the

world or anything contained in the world. They're about just being a part of the world, no matter how insignificant.

No matter.

Any matter is better than none.

10

I FOCUS ON MYSELF, PULLING INTO THE WORLD LIKE zooming into an online map, and look for something familiar. The location, the way that version of me moves and speaks and interacts, the scar under my eye, anything. I expect that Wendell has been on the move, but I have no idea how far or for how long. He'd still be easy to spot. He's the only version of me that can break through walls and destroy entire buildings with his mind. That makes him unique among all other variations.

Regardless of how hard I concentrate, there's no way to know which world will appear through this window. Not much of a choice . . . again. An effort, no matter how infinitesimal, is better than sitting around living in some meaningless fantasy world. Not like I don't have the time to look anyway. I have nothing but time here. Time and possibilities.

In one world I see my birth parents. Wrong. In another I see myself giving a presentation in front of a classroom. Doubt it. I'm buying cigarettes with a fake ID. Not a chance. I'm driving what looks like a brand new car. He wouldn't care. I'm in a swimming pool. No. I'm at a computer watching a video of two women—not that one. I seem to be missing a finger. Not likely. Trying to change the diapers on a crying baby. No way. I look over a small crowd from the stage of an art gallery. Next.

I see an office and a woman talking to me about properly organizing client contracts. On to the— wait. I know her. Ms. Sheridan, I think. My boss in the world where I was a law office intern and my parents divorced. She nods. "Got it?" she asks.

"Got it," I say.

"Knew you would."

The change could be somewhere else. Like maybe I have a different position in the firm in this reality, or I was referred by a different person. There's got to be some places where these worlds overlap. There's enough of them. Nevertheless, it's not my world. Move on.

"Odin." I hear Evelyn behind me. "Why are you doing this?" Her voice quivers as she speaks.

In the next world, I see the interior of a car from the backseat. There are couple of people I don't know, one girl and one boy, in the driver and passenger seats. The girl leans her head around the backrest. "Hey, Odin," she says, "check it out." She pulls a nine-milimeter from the glove compartment. She makes a poking motion while yelling, "Bang, bang, bang!" The gun goes off. The bullet hits the seat next to me. "Oh god!" she yells, dropping the gun as she covers her mouth. Not mine. Moving on.

"Why do you want to hurt me?" Evelyn says. But she's not Evelyn. She's an approximation of her. A hollow shadow of the Evelyn that I know. "All I want is for you to love me," she says, voice cracking.

"Leave me alone," I growl.

I'm in the hall of a school I don't recognize. There are cracks in the ceiling and paint peeling off the walls in sheets. I hear myself yelling at some other kid, stepping in front of him as he tries to maneuver past me. Others in the hallway watch. My face comes incredibly close to him, so close I can count his eyelashes when he looks down and turns away. "The fuck you think you're going?" I say loudly, seeing small globs of bubbly, white spit land right on his face. That's not me. Moving on.

"Look at me, please," says the voice behind me. "Please," she says again, "I'm begging you."

I'm sitting in the living room of a house, my house in this world, in front of a giant television, the type at the front of the home electronics section in stores. The picture is sharper than real life. It's a nature documentary, tigers in the wild, every individual hair visibly bending in the wind. There's a fireplace to the left and a full-sized statue of a man riding a horse on the right. This is a possibility. I wouldn't put it past Wendell to use his power—my power—to take something like this.

"This is boring." I hear a voice whine from somewhere nearby. I look over.

"Shut up," I say. "You might learn something." I see a young girl making a face at me, Zisa, the sister I could have had. Time to move on.

"She'll never need you like I do," Evelyn says. Her voice is colder now. "That's why you brought me here, to experience all the things with her that you never will. To do to me what you can't with her."

Four fingers lightly brush the back of my shoulder. "She'd never let you touch her." I move toward the window and try to focus. One fingernail slides down the side of my neck. "But you can touch me," she whispers, "anytime you want." Her breath warms the skin behind my ear.

"Stop bothering me," I say.

"Anytime. Anywhere. Anything." Her hands press against my shoulder blades. Her lips tickle the back of my neck. I flinch away. This isn't how I want her. "Am I distracting you?"

I shift quickly to pull away from her. "Don't you dare," I growl. "That moment is ours. Hers and mine. Stay away." In the next world, I see nothing but light and dark. I'm blind. Again. "No," I say. The real me, or as real as unreality gets. I shake my head. I know it. I feel it. It's happening.

"She doesn't deserve you," says the imaginary person running her hand over my head, whispering into my ear when I least want it, another voice that won't stop talking.

"Shut up," I say.

"You know that she fucked Kevin, right? I mean, that's what he said." Fingers move softly on my earlobe.

"Go away."

"In the backseat of his car." Her voice is a breathy whisper. "The windows fogged. She pulled his shirt up to feel his chest."

"Stop. Talking." I leap to my feet and spin to face her. She's crouched like a gremlin greedily dismantling a machine. Her pupils appear painted black.

"He licked the sweat off her neck," she says almost as a curse. "She moaned in his ear."

"Shut! Up!"

"She put her hand down his pants."

"Stop!"

"He took her panties down and pushed her legs apar—"

"Shut the fuck up!" My hand strikes the window.

I feel the floor shake from my voice. The computer monitor on the desk topples over. Picture frames fall and shatter. Books drop to the floor. A crack in the window appears from where I hit it.

"Just," I say, one open palm out front, "leave me alone."

"Why?" Genuine confusion on her face.

"Because you're not real. None of this is real." I glance to the crack in the window. A faintly blue light shines through. "None of it means anything."

"It means something to me."

"You're not real," I say. The dark hair, the button nose, long legs and refined face, she is the better version of Evelyn, except in the ways that matter. "You're nothing."

Her hands come together as though in prayer. She stares from down on her knees. "But I could be anything. I could be everything." Her hands drop to her lap. "I can change," her voice lowers to a rasp. She straightens up, arches her back, presses her chest out. Her breasts expand. The fabric of her shirt stretches to almost bursting. "I can be whatever you want me to be."

I can't stop my head from shaking at her. "No," is all I can say.

"At least let me try." Another tremor shakes the room. The walls groan. "I can make you happy here."

My eyes open wide. I see it all now.

"You did this," I say.

She shakes her head. "No, we did. You and I together."

There's a rumble and the room shakes again, from the outside. Through the window I can see huge clouds of dust chasing rocks crumbling from the sides of the ridgeline. The entire face of one mountain shatters into an avalanche.

"Don't," she says meekly. "Please don't do this." Her fingers grope for my hand. "Stay with me. Please." I ball up my fists. I want to destroy everything.

The mountaintops crush downward. Thick masses of dust explode from rocks tumbling toward the suburbs in the distance. Landslides wipe away the houses and streets at the edge of the town. Buildings tremble violently. They shatter from the top down. The tallest to the smallest, splitting in two before exploding into tiny pieces. The rising dust looks like the gas giants of a long dead universe. The roads crack and splinter. The cars melt away. The people vanish. Plains replace mountains. The rim of the city rushes forward as though falling off the edge of the world.

"Please don't," she begs.

Ben and Aida are gone. Andre too. Our house. Brent, Richard, Maria, Kevin as the friend he could have been, everyone else. No more. Creations of a lonely, desperate mind. No matter.

"You're ruining it!" Tears shine on her face. "Everything I made!" she screams. Cracks break from the corners of her eyes to the sides of her head. "My work! My world!" Her hair fractures and falls, her arms and ears next. "You're ruining it all!"

She explodes into jagged pieces. A hollow shell

and nothing more. Nothing left but the room I came here in, with blank book spines, vaguely defined furniture, and a floor to ceiling window with nothing behind it but darkness. A blue-tinged light leaks through one crack. I place my palm against the glass. It shatters.

A light blinds me. A hundred lights. A million shafts of a million lights. Huge twisting and branching structures reach upwards like vines in an ancient, overgrown forest. They're several thousand times taller than I am. They intersect, split, join, arch, and weave their way up to a canopy of hazy light. Some light streams end before the others. Between them is nothing. Emptiness. They are infinite lights in eternal dark.

A root structure winds away in every direction below my feet. Its lights fade as the paths deepen. Above the rising structures all meet a layer of fog or dust before splitting outward, like the roots below. I can barely see the lights beyond that point.

I take a step. I don't feel anything beneath my

feet but I still move forward, drawing closer to one upward stream of lights. Individual points seem to descend without moving. Or no. The points aren't moving. The beam is growing, very, very slowly but noticeably from down here. New points appear just outside of the haze which pulls ever away. I reach out to touch one of the lights in front of me, a single point in a straight column-like struct—

A boy screams as a large dog digs its fangs into his arm. Another boy backs away in panic. The dogs growls, shaking the arm in its teeth. The boy kicks at it. Blood streams from the punctures.

—I bring my hand away.

A scene from another life. Was it one of mine? Maybe someone else. A tragic event in some other person's life. Those were always the easiest to find when looking through someone else's history.

"This is you?" I say out loud, still hearing myself. "Eden?"

Her response isn't a voice anymore. It appears

in my head, the way it did when I first arrived in the office. "You destroyed it all."

"Are these the worlds? The way they really are?" I move from the straight column to another, a short stump which veers wildly before ending. I picture myself before placing my hand on the top.

My fingers are small and stubby, like a baby's. I'm in a car seat with my feet sticking out in front of me. I see bright blue Velcro shoes with lightning bolts on them. My mother is in the driver's seat. She looks down to me and reaches one finger out. I grab it in my tiny hand. A car horn makes my mom turn away. The screech of brakes. I fly forward. And then nothing.

I remove my hand from the top of the truncated world. I trace my eyes over the lights of other worlds that continue on. Some fork off in several places before following their own paths, at times parallel to each other, at times diverging greatly. Others meet somewhere and move forward as one.

I feel the words again. "I just wanted you to be happy here."

I was a child in that world, up until I died. "These are my lives," I say aloud. I look down at the bottom, where the roots gather into the beginning of one upward column. That must be the past. I crane upward to the layer of haze where every structure, be they columns or vines or trunks or whatever else, seems to reach at the same point. Behind this place, very little is clear. The future is still being constructed.

"You have no idea how lonely it is here," Eden says into my head.

There's a term for that, the point at which light from a black hole will never reach beyond, like the future or the horizon. I know I read this somewhere, probably while not doing the homework I was supposed to do.

"I never knew what lonely was until you arrived."

Event horizon! That's it. Light on one side never escapes while objects on the other appear to stand still. The point of no return. It's not an exact parallel but it feels good enough. At least I was able to remember it.

"But that changed because of you." I say nothing. I keep staring at that line between now and later. A line that's always there, just ahead, but never reached, never seen, never ending. Until it does. Her words become a low rumble in my head. "I gave you everything you wanted. Used your memories to craft the perfect life." It feels as though my skull could split apart from the inside. "I could have given you things you could never imagine. Built worlds beyond anything your reality would allow."

The front right of my brain is about to burst. "You have no idea what we could have done together. The places you could see. The pleasures you could experience. The energy we had together. It was unlimited." I drop to my knees. I press my hands to my head as though they're the only things keeping it together. "Energy means nothing without a mind to guide it. Without an intelligence to structure and shape it.

"It's not real," I whisper between gritted teeth.

"Instead of appreciating all I could do with you. For you. You rejected it."

"It's not real."

"You destroyed it."

"Then let me leave!" I yell.

The rumbling begins to settle. The throb in the front part of my brain fades.

"Place me in exile and go back to how things were before," I say, rubbing at last vibrations from beneath my skull.

"How can I?" The words are gentler. As they were in the room. "How am I supposed to go back to being unaware after being conscious? How can I give up being alive?"

"Because that's part of life," I say. I look again at the point where the known present meets the unknown future. "Everything ends eventually."

"Not me."

"Even you," I reply. "You said there is only the present. That means you won't notice if there was a past or a future or huge gaps in between. Maybe I wasn't the first one here. Maybe this has happened before."

I regain my footing.

"If it's worth anything, Eden, I am sorry." It feels weird being the one to say it this time. "I didn't understand what was happening or what you were doing. But the truth is, no matter what you do, I'll never be content with a life here."

"Why?"

"Because I'm human. It's in our nature to never be content." She's quiet again. The lights really do go on forever in every direction. Infinity. Even here the concept seems foreign.

"What do you want, Odin? What do you want most?"

"I just want to go home. I want to keep my friends, the people I care about, the world as I know it, safe. None of them deserve to suffer because of me."

"Or you could bring them all here."

"It's not the same. There are no stakes here. No risks and no consequences. As awful as those things may be they're . . . they're kinda what makes living worth the effort. You have to get it right the first time because there's no reset button. Not for them." I can't imagine Evelyn and my parents and Andre and Brent suffering because of me. I actually can't. The images don't come. "Besides," I say after a pause, "I can't be a prisoner again."

"You're not a prisoner, Odin."

"And if I am going to be a prisoner, I want to see the walls."

"You were supposed to be a partner."

The solid ground of the past, the unreachable boundary of the future, and the infinite vertical lines of the present—I was wrong. These spans aren't columns or vines or anything of the sort. They're bars. Bars meant to keep me here.

"I won't play anymore," I say. "I won't feed you. So, your choice. Either you help me leave and you go back to existing without consciousness, or I'll stay but be completely useless to you and you'll feel every moment as a waste. Up to you."

I sit down. I hug my knees to my chest and let my head slump forward. An overdramatic gesture in the real world, but here it feels about right.

"You won't rot, Odin. You'll let me use your mind one more time. Once more and never again."

"For what?"

"To find your home."

11

SHE TELLS ME TO PICTURE SOMETHING UNIQUE TO MY world, a time that stands out in my mind would be easiest. She doesn't want to specify a tragedy, but I know exactly what she means.

"I found you," appears in my mind, "I'll take you there."

―――――⌄―――――

Mom holds my hand as we walk through the lobby of our apartment building. Metal mailboxes line one wall, while the other wall has a window of thick glass with a small opening at the bottom, a few feet away from a door marked "Staff Only." A man with graying hair, small glasses and a high-collared uniform sits behind the window.

"Good morning, George," he says.

My father nods to him. "Hey, Jerry."

"Have a good day at school, Odin," Jerry says, looking at me through the window that separates him from the lobby. He smiles and waves.

"Say 'hi' to Jerry," says Mom. She stops for me to say "hi." I look up at her, seeing mostly the bottom of her chin, then the slivers of her pale eyes, the same color as mine. "Say 'hi,' sweetie," she says. I say nothing.

"I guess he's shy today," Mom says.

"It's all right. Have a good day as well, Rose."

"You too, Jerry."

We turn to where George, Dad, has already reached the main entrance of the apartment building, a pair of heavy doors with large windows looking onto the street. He opens the door and the light is almost blinding. We step outside and the door shuts behind us. There's the street, the curb, the tarp over the front of the building across from ours, the memory I've never been able to see before.

Then the whole world starts to shake. My vision trembles to a blur. "Odin," I hear my mother say, "Odin, are you are all right?" My head angles down. My free hand quakes. My legs almost give out. It's as though an electrical current has suddenly taken over my entire body. It's not painful, but not pleasant.

There's the traffic. The other people on the street. There's Dad turning in front of us, coming back. He bends down to try to steady my shoulders. Mom steps toward the road, traffic only inches behind her. There's concern behind the hands covering her face.

"Odin," I hear my dad say. My head shakes so much that he has ten eyes and five noses.

"No," I hear another voice say, mine. "Not here."

Suddenly my legs, arms, chest, neck, and head

go stiff. My father jolts forward as though pushed from behind, or pulled from the front.

"Not now," I hear myself say. "Not now."

I see the energy ripple through the air in front of me, shoving my father back, my mother behind him, too far behind him. She screams. She's falling. My dad turns and leaps out to try to reach her. The high heel of Mom's shoe scrapes against the side of the curb. Her hands and fingers grope the air. Her eyes fill with equal parts confusion and horror. Dad pivots to grab her. He leans with one foot off the ground. He catches her at the wrist. He strains to pull. His weight hangs off balance. He can't bring her in. They both fall.

The truck appears out of nowhere. Brakes screech. Tires skid. Steering wheel turns. Inertia continues. My father's face bounces off the grill of truck as my mother rolls underneath it. The truck stops there. One tire is on the curb. And then all is still.

"No." The driver's knuckles are white with

pressure. "Not this." There's a scratch on the end of Mom's heel. "Not now." Dad's arm hangs off the curb. "Not again." The silver grill of the truck shines around the red splatters. "No."

The first scream comes from across the road. The second from above me. The third, fourth and fifth, I can't tell. Cries of shock. Cries for help. Cries for an ambulance. Everyone is crying. Everyone except for me. The silver grill is almost white on the top and almost black at the bottom. It's a net of metal crosses. A single drop of blood falls from one thread to another, sits there, accumulates, and falls to the next.

"Oh my god!" I hear from right behind me. I spin to see Jerry standing there, his uniform wrinkled around the midsection.

"What is it?" I say, looking up at him.

He's pale and frozen, as though he's just seen a ghost.

An intense light flows from the life in front of me at the exact point where the column takes an almost ninety-degree cut about one-third of the way up. Then another extreme glow at the heart of another turn before a steady, although occasionally bumpy, rise. Every bump is dotted by a particularly bright point. There are no other branches or twists up to the haze between now and later.

"This is you," the vibrations in my head say. "This is your world."

The nearest lives around it are short stumps no more than half the length of this one. It's like the last tree standing after the chainsaws come through, scarred from an attempt to cut it down.

"You're linked to this world," she says. "Inextricably."

"An anomaly," I say.

"The fact that you don't belong is what makes you special here."

"Just like Wendell." I lean very close to the spot of deviation but don't touch it. It's an infinitely small dot of dark in the center. The light ripples around it like a vortex.

"You're a leak for energy to flow through."

"What happens if there's no more leak?"

"Can't be done from here."

"From there?" I ask.

"I don't know. It could either plug the hole or reverse it."

"Reverse it?"

"Yes. You are a product of that world, so your presence there could be ordinary. But you have also been here, so there may be some lasting effects."

"So I'm either ordinary or extraordinary?" No answer. "Is that what happened to him?"

There's a delay in her response. "This is all new to me."

I nod. "Me too."

The other bright points don't appear to have the same rippling effect, at least not that I can see. "Well," I say, glancing at how the stream of my life flows straight ahead, "looks like I have no choice." I look up at point there the haze fades. I reach out for it.

"Just because you can see the world doesn't mean you can enter it," she says.

"I have to start somewhere."

"There you are."

Bits of snow cling to the glass in front of me. The street outside is covered in a thin layer of white, the sidewalk and road still visible under and between the snowflakes.

"I was wondering when you'd find your way back."

There's a series of newspaper boxes and a metal trashcan chained to a no parking sign along the curb. Footprints and tire marks indent the shallow snow.

"Welcome."

It was summer when I left. Has it been that long? Or maybe longer. Maybe years.

"No need to be so quiet," Wendell says, turning away from the window toward the interior of a well-furnished studio apartment. There is a multi-level desk with a laptop on it plugged into a printer on the floor and a tablet on the side. A kitchen with a refrigerator, oven, stove top, and a pair of faucets that all sparkle. The kitchen island looks like it's covered in marble. "I can feel you there," he says, "I know exactly where you are."

It was you that day.

"You're going to have to be more specific." He turns quickly to the other side of the room. I see the door to the bathroom and then a pair of couches and floor lamps in front of several bookshelves. Only a few books remain, toppled on their sides haphazardly. I don't recognize the few covers I can see from here.

The day they died. You killed them.

"That is not true," he says.

I saw it!

"You saw one side, Odin. Your side. That is all you ever see."

On the other side of the room, in front of the door, is a large pile of books tossed from the shelves. They're thrown to the floor with covers open and pages bent. A few pens stick upright. Under the pile, one shoe slightly overlaps another. The rest of the body peeks between pages and covers. Chest up, face down, fingers mangled on one hand. "That is why you never understood."

Murderer.

"You cannot kill what was never alive, Odin. Nor can you kill that which cannot die. In either case, I am anything but a murderer. I am a liberator. I am here to give this world freedom from the tyranny it lives under, both from the arbitrary forces which decide the future of so many helpless people, and from the notion that this life is all they have. This world is mine now, Odin. You no longer have a place here."

No. You're the anomaly. You're the one who

entered my world. The one who made me into an outsider. I belong there.

"This was my world first. But it was too flawed. It needed to be remade. I swore it would be different. I waited for my chance. I watched empires rise and fall. Violence. Chaos. I saw people suffer and die for nothing. And I learned that there is only one true agent of change in this world. Terror. That is how people learn. I tried to assist you in this lesson, Odin, even allowed you to experience it firsthand. But you never could understand anything other than yourself. Thus you, usurper, had to be done away with. George and Rose—my parents—they died because you were trying to deny my world to me."

You caused it. Your presence changed my life. You opened the path in my mind. You changed me.

"No, Odin, you made me change. If you hadn't—"

Bullshit. He laughs. I don't feel it.

"Is that the best you can do?"

Not even close.

"Show me then. Show what you have learned during your time away. What skills have you acquired? Go ahead." He places his hand—my hand—into my sight. The fingers bend limply, "If you belong in this world, return to it. Return as simply as I did." I tell the fingers to move. I order the muscles to flex, twitch, convulse, make any movement at all. Nothing happens. "I thought so."

He turns back to the window. A couple in thick coats and knit caps stride confidently down the sidewalk. A black sedan rides along the road cautiously.

"I know you have seen them. Those other worlds. How random they are. How arbitrary the universe is." The sedan on the road draws closer to the couple on the sidewalk. "The way things happen for no reason. How one little stumble can make the difference between life and death." Wendell places his fingers on the glass as the couple passes him. The car increases its speed. "Random and yet, repeating."

You wouldn't.

"Of course not." The car passes the couple. "There would be no purpose in their sacrifice. In my world, there is no war, no poverty, no wondering why good things happen to some while bad things happen to others. In my world, you know that you are one of many, a small part of a bigger entity. You do not fear the future. Rather, you embrace all its possibilities."

And this is how it starts? Home invasions?

He laughs again. "Progress is being made. Obstacles are falling," he points to the body under the books. "As expected, your friend the doctor and her colleagues have not ceased their pursuit of a weapon that could rival me. I have already stopped them at another location."

It's true. Six weeks ago. It happened at another underground facility in another part of the country, some place warm even in the fall. He came to the base at night. He walked right through the front gate. The guards were nothing—

"Odin," he says, "I can feel you snooping. These are not your memories anymore."

He turns toward the front of the apartment. The man's every finger is snapped. His elbows and knees are bent backward. His feet face the opposite way of the body. Chest up, face down. "This one," he says, "was working on yet another. I tracked him down. I learned what he knew. Then I made sure he saw the error in his ways before he paid for them."

Monster.

"No. The real monsters are the ones who want to control the world through a power that does not belong to them. The ones who usurp power for their own means. I am using what I was given, the power that I tried to guide you in to reshape this world, until you proved unworthy. So it falls again to me to build something better for everyone. Otherwise, there is no point in having power."

Monster.

"No more so than you, Odin. Have you not figured this out yet? We are the same. Two different possibilities with the same capacity for greatness. Only you are the older version while I am the update. I am the one who learned about the world, about the people in it. I recognize that the only way to unite people is through a common threat. I am sure you know this as well, but you do not want to admit it. No one ever does. Well, since no one else is capable, I will become that threat."

Solar Flare.

"Precisely. I will show them their destruction. Destruction will guide them toward salvation. Toward me."

You're sick. I see the room sway as he turns and paces through it.

"No, Odin, you are. To have this power and not use it is negligence of the highest order. Only a true monster would allow the chaos of this world to continue when you have a way to end it."

Not through death.

"Through knowledge, knowledge that they are not alone, that they are not finite creatures. But, to teach them anything, first you must establish authority. You must show that you are greater than they are, using the only terms they understand." There's vague reflection in the window. He looks somehow smaller than I remember.

How?

"You are a smart kid, Odin." I can imagine the sneer as he speaks. Too bad I can't feel it. "Figure it out for yourself."

I feel myself shoved out from his mind. I'm flung from the apartment, the building, the city, the country, the planet, the universe. The lights of the column swirl in front of me. Countless tiny galaxies spiral in the distance.

"What did you find?" Eden asks.

"Myself," I reply. "The worst version of myself."

12

EVELYN HAS ONE PICTURE ON THE WALL OF HER BEDROOM: a black and white photograph of a woman swimming underwater as the camera sits directly at surface level. The coral and sand beneath the water is as visible in the foreground as the beach and mountains are in the background. The picture is framed and mounted on the wall opposite of her bed with its thick, purple comforter and three of the eight candy-colored pillows still in place on top of it.

She paces between the foot of the bed and the wall with the photograph. Laptop and phone sit on the comforter, just out of reach, as she turns to start her walk across the room again. Her baggy t-shirt swings with the motion, hanging long enough that it almost covers the tight running shorts. Her right hand gestures freely while the left holds up a well-worn collection of papers with two horizontal creases dividing it into thirds. Her lines are highlighted in green.

She keeps her eyes up at the ceiling while walking. Her character reads an encyclopedia entry about how her husband will die that day from a mountain climber's axe lodged into his skull. Her husband, whose lines she lips over for pacing, dies at the end of the scene, and then over and over at the end of every reoccurrence of that scene throughout the course of the short play. The theatre teacher, Mrs. Bourne, has already promised Evelyn several different parts in the school's winter production, a showcase of one act plays. Evelyn's favorite is this one, the husband and wife doing several variations on how he will die that day by having an axe plunged into his skull. She does her best 1950s sitcom tone to explain that maybe the gardener needed to "axe" him something and then laughs.

Her phone rings. She stretches out to the reach for it, one long leg extended into the air while the other tightens to balance, like a gymnast or a ballerina. I wonder why she doesn't show her legs off more. I can see the name on the phone. Brent.

"Hey," she says.

He's leaning back in the office chair at the desk in his room, feet up on his bed, an online scoreboard on the computer. "Hey," he says back. "How's practice?" I switch between them, like flipping channels.

"It's fine." She pushes the laptop away and sits down, bouncing slightly on the mattress. "It's not really this show that I'm concerned about."

"Yeah?" he says. His voice is pitched higher than usual.

"Yeah. It's the one next semester. If I can nail each of these parts, it'll give me a big advantage in my Ophelia audition."

"Well too bad for everyone else, because none of them have a chance."

She smiles. "That's sweet."

"Yes, it is, but it's also true."

"What are you doing?"

Brent looks at the lists of kills, deaths, head-shots, and so forth on the screen in front of him. "Just finished studying."

"Which class?"

"Bio."

"Kinda glad I got that class out of the way last year."

"Yeah, well, I'd ask you to help me study, but I think there are other things we'd rather do together."

She smiles shyly. "Yeah."

I need to look away.

"Are you free again Friday?"

"I dunno." One side of her mouth curls up. "What do you want to do?"

I have no right to look into her life, or his.

"Not study for biology."

I have no claim to either of them. I don't even have a place in their world anymore.

"That sounds very nice." Her voice is something between a purr and a growl.

I need to stop. It's too much. I pull away. I see the dull brown roof of her house, the small back yard with the old swing set.

He had a crush on her but gave it up when we became friends. That's the rule: you don't like the girl one of your friends likes. Maybe whatever is happening started because I wasn't there. They'd talk about me, I saw that before, wonder where I was and what happened. They talked a lot about it for the first few weeks.

The whole school did at first, especially while Eric and Dylan and them were out at the same time. We'd all been kicked out for fighting. We were all sent to juvenile. We were all in the hospital. Once those guys came back, refusing to talk about the incident under threat of immediate detention of them and their families from Choi and his entire squad of agents, I was now alone in their eyes. I was the only one kicked out, sent to juvie, in the hospital hooked to breathing machines with doctors deciding whether or not I could be saved. My family suddenly left town to escape all the attention I was getting. I was abducted by aliens, we all were in fact, but the others managed to get away. The stories became little worlds of their own.

Brent even tried to get in contact with my parents but didn't know how. He'd give updates to Evelyn every couple of days. Tried calling my phone but no answer, sent texts but no answer, messaged on Facebook but no answer. The phone number was canceled soon thereafter. Brent and Evelyn would frown together and wonder what happened and wish things were different. He'd say that she, of course, was completely without fault and shouldn't be sad.

"I'm sure he's fine," he'd say. "Odin'll be in touch when he's ready." He never told her about leading me through that door into the lions' den. "You know Odin," he said. "He's always been kinda quiet and careful about what he shares." It was through this concern that he and Evelyn bonded. Because he's the nicest guy ever, and there was no reason he couldn't like her. I should be happy for them, if they are. Still . . . I don't . . . I don't want to think about this anymore.

A large pizza box awaits in the middle of the coffee table in front of the television. Three bowls of salad on three sides of the box. Andre sits on the floor in the middle, Aida on one side of the couch behind him.

There's a *Simpsons* rerun on. I can't tell which

episode it is. Probably one of the newer ones I haven't seen as often, or possibly ever. It's been a while since I've been able to watch anything that didn't already exist in my head.

"Can you bring a knife and some napkins too, hon?" Aida calls over her shoulder to Ben in the kitchen.

"For what?"

She rolls her eyes. "You know for what," she says.

Ben looks down at Andre as he returns. "She'll never learn," Ben says.

"Learn what?"

"How to eat pizza," Ben answers. He hands Aida her knife and a few napkins before putting the rest on the table. The hairs on Ben's chin are mostly white.

"I don't like getting my fingers all greasy," she says.

"Grease is part of the fun of pizza."

"Yeah, Mom, it's not pizza if it isn't greasy," Andre says, pushing the salad aside and grabbing for two slices.

"Not for me."

Ben hands her a plate with one slice. She dabs the napkin on top of the piece until the napkin is almost see-through. I remember her doing that only once before. We didn't eat much pizza, and never while watching television.

"And you should be a bit more careful about that as well," she says. Ben glances over at her but she's already looked away. His neck lacks the definition it had the last time I saw him. His belly hangs farther out than I remember.

"All right," he taps Andre's shoulder, "here's how we eat pizza the right way."

"There's no wrong way to eat," Aida says, slicing a bite with her knife.

"Don't listen to her, my son, she's a bad influence." She makes a face at him. Andre laughs. "This is how we do it in New York," he says in an accent that sounds like it's from anywhere other than New York.

"When were you ever in New York?" Aida asks.

"Last week when I was watching *Taxi Driver*, now quiet down while I teach our son one of the fundamentals of life."

"That's a sad life," she mutters.

"A life filled with pizza is never sad. Short maybe, but not sad." Andre laughs again. "Anyway, here's how we do it in New York. You take the pizza like this and then you fold it over like this." He presses the two ends of the crust close to each other. "And then you bite it." He takes a bite. Andre does the same. "And then," he says, still chewing, "you like drive around with Jodie Foster and talk to yourself in the mirror. Something like that, I dunno, I've never been to New York."

Andre laughs. Aida closes her eyes and shakes her head. "This kid is doomed," she mutters.

Andre turns back to the television as he takes another bite from his folded pizza. The framed photo of us remains next to the set. It's the four us at Trout Beach, Ben and I soaking wet, Andre with a big, cheesy smile, and Aida cringing as Dad pulls her against him. It's the only indication I can find that I ever existed in this house.

Ben and Aida barely spoke about me for the last few months. Even in their room before sleeping. The first several days, it was constant questions from Aida: What are they doing with him? When can we see him? Do you know where he is? Is he okay? Followed by a steady stream of I don't know, I don't know, I only know what they tell me, I don't know. It eventually became so repetitive, so routine and hopeless that they both just stopped talking about it. Better to think of me as gone for good. For Andre, I was off at college. That was good enough. They moved on.

Nobody even told them that I'd escaped. The project was continuing exactly as planned. Anything different would be admitting failure.

Worse yet, as Director Braxton explained to Choi and others from the Project, any news of what happened at Fort Colton would cause questions the Project did not want to answer. Better to keep it quiet. No need to create panic when the danger would be over soon. He will be caught, Braxton said, quickly. That was four months ago. Dr. Burnett was not there. She was busy being held under house arrest while awaiting trial.

Wendell stared up at the light through the water. The wet lake floor soaked through the thin slippers. He knew I was gone, pushed away, but still connected, still feeding him enough power. He started walking, every step sinking and coming up with more sand and sediment falling into the gap between his foot and his footwear. This is how he escaped. After tearing through a legion of soldiers, ripping a weapon of mass destruction apart from the inside out, and holding back tons of surging water, he had to slog across a waterlogged lake bed for an hour before finally reaching the shore on the far side of the fort he'd just escaped from. Not a particularly badass way to begin his reign.

He waited until after dark to continue. Even if the orange uniform still stood out, at least he wouldn't be wandering through an upscale lakeside neighborhood in a prison jumpsuit in the middle of the day. Keep your head down and walk with a purpose and people tend to assume you belong there, unless they have their own reasons to think you don't. Luckily, no one called the police. Lucky for them. There's no doubt that the cops would have opened fire on him, being in that neighborhood, looking as he did. They probably would have died for it.

He disabled the security cameras before breaking into a clothing store. Stole some basic items and went off, taking whatever he needed on his way. He knew they'd be searching for him in the immediate area, or anywhere around people I knew from the base or life before. Ben and Aida, my classmates, Dr. Burnett, Choi, anyone at all whom I'd ever had contact with would already be under surveillance. He had to find another way to get the information he needed. Quietly. Prepare. Once the weapon was no longer a threat, then he'd make his move. He'd let the whole world know of his presence. Show them just how small and pointless they were. Not yet. Once the threat was gone . . .

I sit with my back to the world that I came from, a world changed radically by my presence, whether the people who live there know it or not. I twisted it. I made it differ from its original path. It might have been Wendell's work that caused that change but I still allowed it to happen. My deeds or not, the huge turn in the course of my world is still my responsibility. No one else can fix the forces we anomalies have unleashed on their world. No one else should have to suffer because of our mistakes, either.

Ben and Aida might have been ordered to take me in, but they still did it. Andre admired me despite my disinterest. Evelyn was always so sweet, so harmless, so deserving of happiness. Brent works so hard to make everyone like him. As manipulative as her plans may have been, Dr. Burnett's motivation was still good. Even Kevin doesn't deserve the danger that Wendell promises to bring. There may be some in the world who do, murderers and rapists and bigots, people with evil intentions, but most people, those who just try to be decent while having the best life they can, they don't deserve to live with such terror.

"I have to go back," I say out loud, to myself. "I have to."

"I know," says Eden.

"For them."

"I know," she says again. Even though she doesn't speak in words, there's still a hint of sorrow.

"I broke this world. I have to fix it." No reply. "This world is a part of you as well," I say, to her this time, the new voice in my head. "A small, insignificant part, but a part nonetheless. You too have some responsibility for it." Silence.

I stand. I look around at the incalculable columns stretching to the ceiling above me. The stumps of short lives, the branches of big decisions, the twists and turns of unexpected events, all the different variations stemming from a common origin. I look up at the receding canopy overhead and speak as though talking to the future.

"You may not admit it," I say, "but you are a guardian of these worlds. Without the lives contained within them, then you, this place, this realm or space between or whatever you call yourself, would not exist. You weren't aware before, but now you are, and this is your chance to preserve some of the lives that sustain you."

I'm not sure what to expect as a response. Maybe

more vibrations in my head. Maybe for Eden to reappear as a little girl. What I get is more nothing.

"I don't know how to get back to my home. You need to help me. You need to help me so I can save this part of you."

"I know, Odin."

"How do I get back?"

"I'll show you."

A flood of images pour into my brain, a process that Eden could never have done without a consciousness to receive them. It would be impossible without an intelligence to interpret her energy into thought. She tells me this. She tells me to find an empty space, the way I did when I first started using my powers. Most of the world is empty space. Even objects that appear solid have space between the atoms in their composition. She says to hold an image of myself in my mind and find an emptiness. She will do the rest.

"You may no longer be an anomaly there," she warns.

"Thank you," I tell her in thought.

I remember those first few weeks of practicing on my own, before Wendell returned. There I am sitting on my floor. There I am, on the floor, one hand up with the fingers slowly curling under the book hovering inches off the carpet. I'm different now, shaved head, possibly leaner after all those training sessions and set meals. One word appears in my mind.

Farewell.

It's dark.

Then the shapes start to appear: solid lines and hard angles and small curves. Corners, wheels, a chair, a desk, a bed. My chair, desk, and bed. I feel the air on my outstretched hand. There's the carpet beneath me. I sit up and pat my thighs. I feel the pressure, the push, the texture, the skin. I'm in my room again. It's all real.

"Yeah!" I hear myself yell, echoing off the walls, shaking my ear drums. "Yeeeeeaaaah!" throwing my arms up.

I jump to my feet. I slap my hand over my heart. I hear the hollow thud and feel the vibration through my chest. My skin is warm and dry and . . . "Shit!" Clothes! I forgot to picture clothes!

The room is cleaner than when I left it. I yank open the drawers and dig through for something to wear. Undies and sweats and a shir—

I hear the spring turning in the doorknob to my bedroom. "Wait," I yell. "Don't!"

The door flies open. I freeze in place with my hands out. The light clicks on.

"Dad?" I say.

I hear, "Don't move."

The barrel of a pistol points at my head.